The Madman of Venice

The Madman of Venice

Sophie Masson

DELACORTE PRESS

This is a work of fiction. Names, characters, places, and incidents either are the product of the author's imagination or are used fictitiously. Any resemblance to actual persons, living or dead, events, or locales is entirely coincidental.

 Published in the United States by Delacorte Press, an imprint of Random House Children's Books, a division of Random House, Inc., New York.
Originally published in hardcover by Hodder Children's Books, London, in 2009.

Delacorte Press is a registered trademark and the colophon is a trademark of Random House, Inc.

Visit us on the Web! www.randomhouse.com/teens

Educators and librarians, for a variety of teaching tools, visit us at www.randomhouse.com/teachers

Library of Congress Cataloging-in-Publication Data
Masson, Sophie.
The madman of Venice / Sophie Masson. — 1st American ed.
p. cm.
ISBN 978-0-385-73843-9 (hc) — ISBN 978-0-385-90729-3 (lib. bdg.)
[1. Missing persons—Investigation—Fiction. 2. Venice (Italy)—Fiction.]
I. Title.
PR9619.3.M2884M33 2010
823'.914—dc22
2009022369

The text of this book is set in 12-point Classic Garamond.

Book design by Angela Carlino

Printed in the United States of America

10 9 8 7 6 5 4 3 2 1

First American Edition

For dear Pippa and Joe,

with love and congratulations

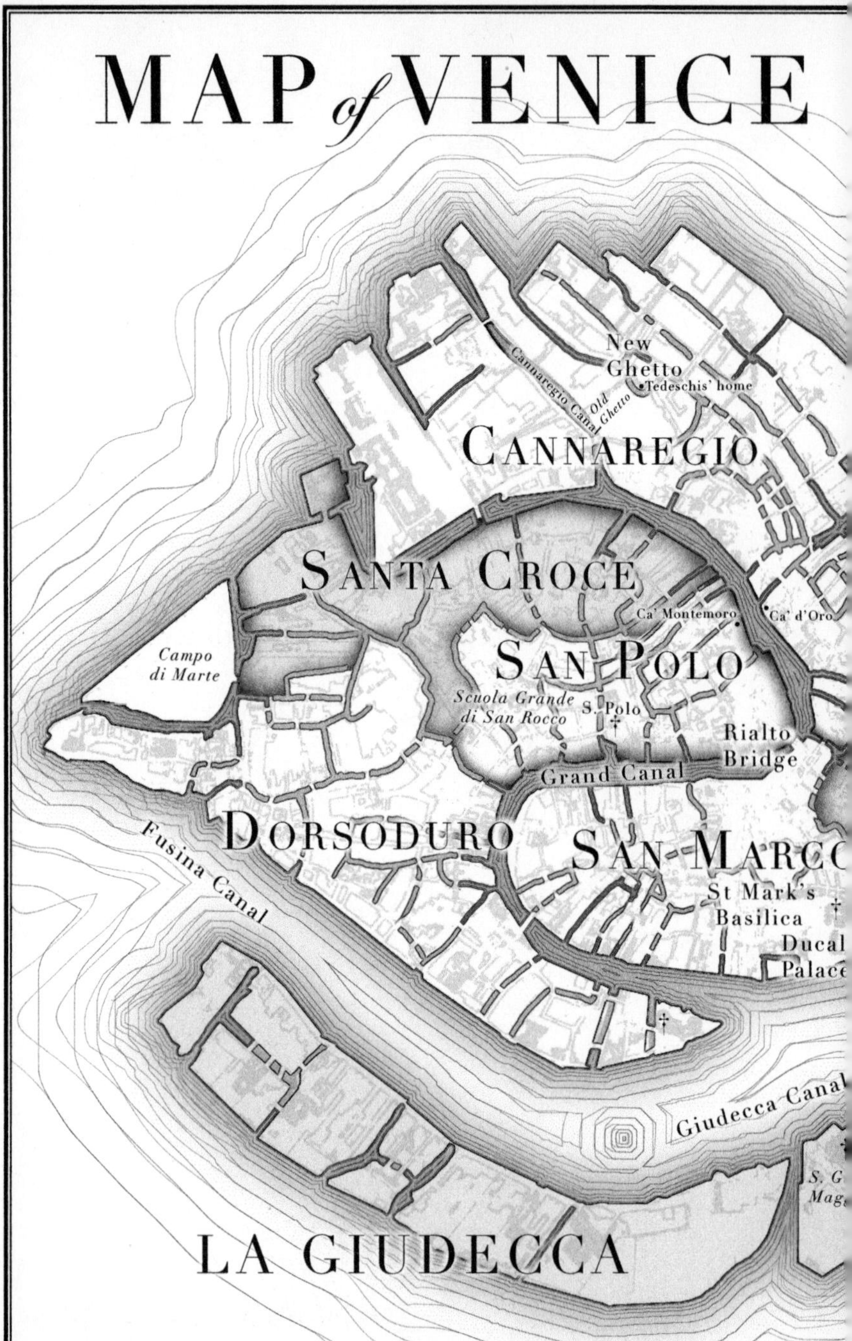

MAP *of* VENICE

New Ghetto
Tedeschis' home
Cannaregio Canal
Old Ghetto
CANNAREGIO
SANTA CROCE
Ca' Montemoro
Ca' d'Oro
Campo di Marte
SAN POLO
Scuola Grande di San Rocco
S. Polo
Rialto Bridge
Grand Canal
Fusina Canal
DORSODURO
SAN MARC
St Mark's Basilica
Ducal Palace
Giudecca Canal
LA GIUDECCA

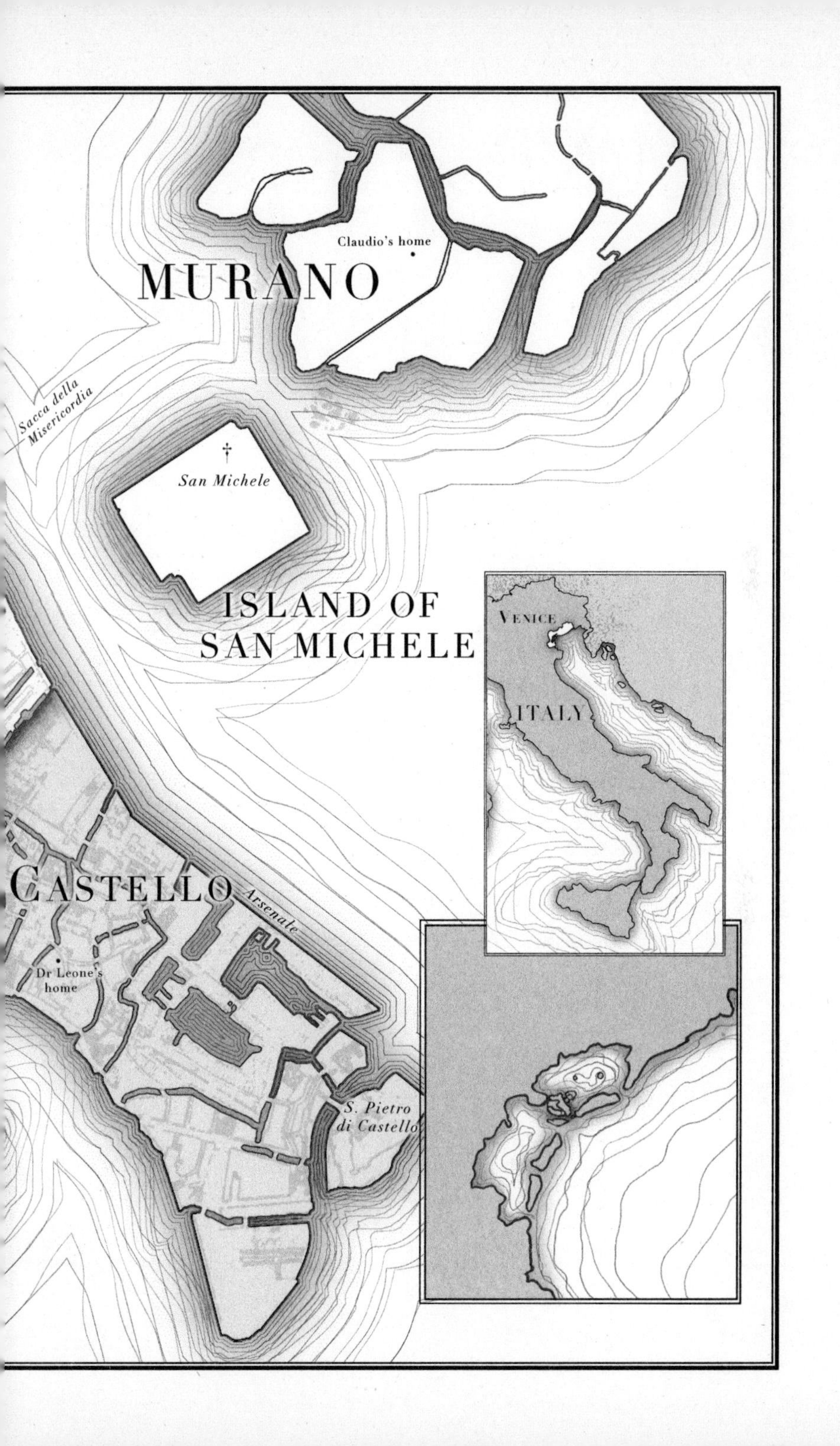

MURANO
Claudio's home
Sacca della Misericordia
San Michele
ISLAND OF SAN MICHELE
VENICE
ITALY
CASTELLO
Arsenale
Dr Leone's home
S. Pietro di Castello

What profit love that cannot show his face?
What profit joy if she doth bring disgrace?
If thou must ask, then thou hast never known
The sweetness and the sorrow that is love's renown.
Now listen well, for here thou will be told
Of darkness, danger, and of lovers bold,
Of poison plots, of vengeance, and of love supreme,
In fairest Venice, where we set our scene.

—from *The Lovers of Venice,* by Edward Fletcher

Prologue

Venice, Carnival

1586

The city is a riot of laughter and parties and noise. Everyone's masked. Everyone's too busy having fun to notice the two young lovers slipping away to the canal backwater, where they can be alone at last, safe from prying eyes.

Taking off their masks, they hold each other tight. The girl says softly, 'I wish . . . how I wish we could be together always,' and the boy says sadly, 'I wish it too, my love, but your father will never—'

She interrupts him, eyes suddenly wide with fright. 'Hush . . . listen. . . .'

Footsteps. Stealthy footsteps. The girl and boy retreat into the shadows, hearts pounding, skin crawling. Have they been followed, after all? The boy clutches the pommel of his sword, thinking: If it's one of his men, I'll sell my life dearly. I will not be taken like a rat in a trap. . . .

Suddenly, the footsteps stop. But no one calls out to the lovers. No one challenges them. No one tries to grab them.

After a moment, they peer out cautiously. There is a man standing on the landing-stage that juts out into the canal. He has his back to them and is of middling height, wearing a long, concealing cloak and hat. One arm is crooked at the elbow, as though he is holding something—a bundle of some sort, though they can't see what it is.

All at once, another sound. Every Venetian knows it like he knows the blood beating in his veins. The steady splashing sound of an oar cutting through water.

There's the gondola now. It's an eerie sight. All black, as the law demands, it's rowed by a tall figure, dressed from head to foot in black. The rower's features are completely concealed by a full-face Carnival mask of a pure, blank, anonymous white. The scene might be some sinister symbolic painting: ferryman Death in his boat, poling slowly to the watcher on the landing-stage . . .

The gondola glides in. The waiting man speaks. His harsh voice carries clearly to the lovers' hiding place. 'You're late. What kept you?'

No answer. The boat is now right beside him. He speaks again. Impatiently. 'It's done. The woman's dead. Now to play your part.'

The rower speaks for the first time. 'I don't like this.' His voice is flat, toneless.

'It's not for you to like or not,' says the other. He holds out his burden and all at once the watchers in the shadows hear a sound that makes their blood run cold. The thin, mewing cry of a newborn baby.

'Take it. Get rid of it, where it won't be found. The lagoon. The sea. Wherever you like.'

The rower's voice rises. 'God's blood, man, this is an innocent child!'

A harsh bark of laughter. 'No one is innocent in this world. God will sort it out in the next. It is not your place to question. Do it. Or perhaps you want to explain yourself to—'

'No!' The flat voice suddenly has an edge of fear in it. 'I never said I wouldn't do it. I only said I didn't like it.'

'Objection noted and dismissed,' says the other man, with a hint of cold laughter. He throws the bundle at the rower, who catches it; there is another thin cry, hastily muffled. Then, without another word, the gondolier puts the baby down in the boat. He takes up his oar again and turns his boat down the canal. As he does so, the moonlight flashes on its prow for just an instant. And in that moment, the boy sees something that makes the hair prickle on his scalp.

As the boat glides away, the watcher looks around him. Seemingly satisfied, he turns on his heels, walks rapidly away up the alley, and is soon gone from sight. Neither of the young people moves, till both boat and watcher have quite disappeared. Only then do they dare to stir.

The girl whispers, 'We must tell what we've seen and heard this night. At once. My father—'

'No! No! We cannot.' He swallows hard. 'We . . . we must forget we saw anything, heard anything.'

She stares at him, uncomprehending. 'Why? They are gone. They did not see us. What danger is there to us now?'

'No. For God's sake . . .' He takes a deep breath. 'Didn't you see that the boat was marked?'

'Marked?'

'Marked with the lion,' he says dully. 'The Lion of Venice. This was a boat from the Duke's fleet. Now do you see, my sweet?'

She shivers. 'No . . . surely . . . no . . . it cannot be. . . . The Duke would never . . . This is monstrous. . . .'

'If it is not the Duke himself, it is someone in his household, in his inner circle. But those men—they had the air of hired swords. Venice is crawling with such men.' He speaks with the authority of experience. 'Hired in secret, on a dark and bloody task. And that means we have blundered into something dangerous. Very, very dangerous. And we must leave it alone. Surely you must see that?'

'But that poor child . . .'

He crosses himself. There are tears in his eyes. 'Its fate is sealed. We can do nothing. Only God can protect it now.'

She cries, 'Oh, darling. I cannot bear it. We must . . . we must leave this terrible place. I cannot bear it any longer. I cannot live here, while such things go on.'

'Then we will leave,' he says, holding her tight. 'We will leave, you and I, for ever.'

She looks at him, her eyes big with fear and grief and horror and longing. 'Yes,' she whispers.

'Will you meet me tomorrow, at our usual place and time?'

She starts. 'So soon?'

'It must be. You must understand that.'

'Then I will try my utmost to be there.'

'I'll wait for you at midday. If you're not there, I'll understand you can't come and I'll wait for you, same time, same place, next day.' He takes her hand and looks into her eyes. 'Promise me you'll tell no one what we saw this night. No one. Not your confessor. Not your cat. Not the walls. No one. Nothing. Promise me?'

She nods, without speaking.

'Think, my sweet. Soon, we'll be away from this accursed place, starting a new life, far from all this.'

'Yes,' she murmurs. 'Yes, yes, my darling, away from all this.' But her words are mechanical and jerky, for her ears are full of that helpless baby's cry.

Part One

A NOBLE VENTURE

London, May 1602

The woman was small and slender, dressed in an unusual shade of deep red that set off her dark, exotic beauty. Under the cowl of her velvet cloak, her sleek jet-black hair was threaded here and there with silver, like filigree in fine velvet. Her large, intelligent brown eyes were set in an oval-shaped face, and she had the kind of skin that would quickly go golden in the summer.

Ned Fletcher was puzzled. She looked like a fine lady—maybe even a lady of the Court. Yet she'd come alone, on foot, without a servant. And she didn't look like a merchant's wife, at least none that he was acquainted with. She had a bold, spirited look that spoke of some other station in life. Not the streets, though. Something he was unfamiliar with.

'Young sir, I wish to speak to Master Matthew Ashby. I understand this is his house.' Her voice was soft and musical and, despite her foreign appearance, very English.

'Yes. It is.'

'Are you his son?' He could see her glance washing over him, taking in all the details of his appearance: the tall, gangly frame, the unruly red hair, the freckled face and green eyes, the shabby clothes. Ned had never been in the glass of fashion. He never could be. He was too untidy. Too poor, also.

He saw she was waiting for an answer. Blushing, he stammered, 'No. I—I'm not his son. I'm Ned Fletcher. His clerk. I'm an orphan. He was kind enough to—'

She cut into his speech. 'I was told your master and his household are leaving for Venice this week. Was I reliably informed?'

Ned stared at her. 'Who wants to know?' he snapped. The trip to Venice wasn't exactly a secret, but it wasn't supposed to be common knowledge either. For Master Ashby was going to Venice as the representative of a group of London merchants. In just over two years he and his colleagues had lost three ships, laden with rich cargoes, to pirates operating off the Venetian coast.

These pirates were particularly cruel and ruthless. Not only did they steal cargoes and ships, they also slaughtered every member of the ships' crews. The London merchants' Venetian agent, Salerio, had been investigating the problems. But three months ago he had been murdered, supposedly by street thieves, before he could complete his investigations. It all stank to high heaven, and the group of London merchants were determined to get to the bottom of it. The only way to really do that was to send someone, undercover, to Venice.

Matthew Ashby had been the obvious choice. He had lived in Venice as a young man, and kept in touch with his best friend there, a famous alchemist by the name of Orlando Leone. It was easy enough for Ashby to go to Venice on the pretext of visiting Leone and showing his family the golden city.

Ned was going too: an exciting fact that had been on his mind for weeks. But he'd been told not to talk about it. And yet now here was this woman, boldly making free with the information. He repeated his question, sharper this time. 'Who wants to know?'

The woman's eyebrows shot up. 'Master Ashby's guard dog has a good barking tongue in his head! Have no fear. I mean no harm. But I make it a practise never to discuss business on the doorstep. Will you not let me in and let him decide for himself whether he should speak to me?'

'Ned, what's wrong?' Celia appeared in the hallway,

her blue eyes alight with curiosity. Ned's heart gave its familiar, hopeless leap.

'This . . . this lady wishes to speak to your father, Celia. But she will not state her business or her name, and your father distinctly said—'

'Miss Ashby,' interrupted the woman impatiently, ignoring Ned, 'you may tell your father that Mistress Emilia Lanier wishes to speak to him on a matter of the greatest importance. Go now. Tell him. See for yourself whether he will speak to me.'

Celia opened her mouth to say something, but thought better of it. Flinging a 'Stay there, Ned' over her shoulder, she hurried off.

'What a very pretty girl,' observed Emilia Lanier with a little smile.

Ned blushed again. 'I . . . I cannot say.'

She laughed. 'Then God has cursed you with blindness, young man.' She leaned towards him and he caught a whiff of her perfume: some heady, musky scent that made his senses reel. 'A piece of advice: both meek sheep and snarling guard dogs repel a lady. Show a lion heart and then you'll win her.'

Ned was scarlet now. How dare she interfere in his personal business! He would have dearly liked to say something cutting in return, but nothing would come. Nothing would, when you wanted it to. Words came easily enough to his quill when he sat in his chamber at night; but would they make their way to his lips? Never. He was too shy, too awkward, too—

At that moment Master Matthew Ashby erupted into the hall. Ned could see at a glance that his master was furious. And with him, most likely—for the glare he directed at Ned would have melted iron. But all he said was 'Mistress Lanier, pray forgive the zeal of my household. Please come in. It is so very kind of you to call.'

'Not at all,' said the woman, swishing past Ned with a tiny wink. Ned swallowed. His master was a good man, but he had a hot temper and he could not suffer fools gladly. *And I suppose I acted like a fool,* thought Ned glumly as he closed the door. *What if . . . what if Master Ashby is so angry he doesn't take me to Venice as he promised?* He'd been looking forward to it so much.

Venice! On one of the walls in Master Ashby's house hung a painting of the fabulous golden city, floating on its lagoon. The painting depicted a Carnival scene with crowds of revellers in fine clothes and masks, and since the first time he had been taken into Master Ashby's household five years ago, Ned had looked at it more times than he could remember, imagining himself amongst that motley crowd. He had also read about Venice in stories and seen it depicted in plays at the Globe Theatre, for the Globe's resident playwright, William Shakespeare, frequently used the city as a setting for his dramas. Ned had so longed to see it in real life, but had never imagined he ever would. . . .

Even more to the point, Celia was coming to Venice too. Chaperoned by Master Ashby's sister, the widowed Mistress Bess Quickly, of course. But that didn't matter. Away from London, away from ordinary life and all the constraints that meant Ned must always appear as a mere clerk, a familiar bit of the furniture to Celia—perhaps he'd have a chance to prove himself to her in a new light. Perhaps he might even make his fortune and win her heart. . . .

Ned didn't learn what Emilia Lanier wanted till a couple of hours later, when Celia barged into the room where he was working on the accounts. Or at least pretending to—for instead of taking down figures, he'd begun jotting down words for another poem about Celia. When she came in, he started violently and quickly covered up his writing. Fortunately, Celia didn't notice. She was too full of her news.

'Ned, I'll wager that you will never guess!'

Rose-cheeked, golden-haired, bluebell-coloured eyes sparkling, slim and graceful in her rustling blue silk dress, she looked to him like a fairy princess, or an angel. But she'd never look at him as a lover . . . never. He was too clumsy. Too tongue-tied. Too poor. Too different from her, with his love of stories and plays and dreams, while she was full of fire and spirit and practicality. But also too *familiar*. She'd known him for years, ever since he was thirteen and she was twelve. Master Ashby had taken him into their household out of family charity, for Ned's dead mother had been some sort of distant cousin to the merchant's own late wife.

At the beginning, Ned and Celia had fought like cat and dog, then found a way to rub along. Now they were easy enough with each other. He knew she had affection for him. But only as a kind of brother or cousin. And until a year or so ago, that's how he'd thought of her. And then things had changed. Something had sparked in his heart . . . something that had quickly grown into a stronger and stronger flame. . . .

Now he said mock-grumpily, 'What should I guess now, flittergibbet? The time of day? The colour of your next dress? Its price, perhaps?'

She pouted. 'Oh, you are a dull dog, Ned, sometimes! If you are going to be like that, I shall not tell you.'

'Tell me what? Oh, do,' he said hastily when she made as if to leave the room. 'I suppose this is about Mistress Lanier.'

'Of course. Who else? She's at the Court. Her husband is a musician in the service of the Queen, and she is a musician and poet herself.'

'Ah, so that is what it was,' said Ned.

'What was what?'

'Why she was different from anyone I'd met,' explained Ned. 'Go on.'

'Her mother was English but her father was a Venetian. A musician too, in the time of King Henry. His surname, I think, was Bassano.'

'How strange. There was a Bassanio in *The Merchant of Venice,*' said Ned, much struck.

'What?' Celia wasn't much of a playgoer.

'Something I saw at the Globe. By that playwright I told you about. Shakespeare.'

'Never mind plays. This is *real* life. Ned, do you remember how Father and his merchant friends were presented to the Queen last summer? Well, Mistress Lanier was one of the musicians at Court. I think Father was rather taken with her.'

'What did she want?' said Ned sharply.

Celia bridled. 'If you're going to be like that . . .'

'Sorry. I did not mean . . . I only meant, if she *is* from the Court, why did she come here in this cloak-and-dagger way? Is she in love with Master Ashby?'

Celia looked at him as though he were mad. 'In love? With *Father*? Don't be silly. She came about a missing girl.'

'What?'

Celia was enjoying herself. She leaned forward, eyes wide, lips parted. Ned had a sudden urge to grab her in his arms and kiss her till she was breathless. 'A girl who's missing in Venice,' she whispered dramatically. 'Her father wrote to Mistress Lanier, asking for help.'

'Why?' said Ned stiffly. *Show her a lion heart and you will win her,* Mistress Lanier had said. God's blood, how did you do that?

'Because he's an old friend of her family. A doctor, who once saved her father's life. This girl is his only child. And Mistress Lanier wants Father to try and find her.'

'Whatever for? Why doesn't she go to Venice herself?'

'Because she can't. It's a delicate matter,' said Celia. 'She can't leave the Court. And her position at Court makes it impossible for her to interfere personally in the matter of this girl, Sarah Tedeschi. Before she disappeared, you see, Sarah ran into serious trouble. She was accused of witchcraft by a powerful Venetian lady.'

Ned's eyes widened. He whistled.

'That's not all,' said Celia, enjoying the effect her words were having on him. 'This Sarah and her father—they're Jews. This Mistress Lanier, she asked Father if that bothered him.'

'I wager I know what he said,' said Ned, who'd heard Master Ashby pronounce on the topic more than once. 'He said that of course he was not bothered, because in his eyes being against the Jews was a sin, for Our Saviour Jesus Christ was born a Jew, as were His family and apostles, and it was a Roman who condemned Him to death. Besides, though some people hate Jewish moneylenders, he thinks that if you borrow money, you must expect to pay it back and not be made a gift of it. Business is business, and he's never been cheated by a Jew. Unlike some Christians he could name.'

Celia laughed. 'Yes. Exactly. He said it all in almost the same words. And Mistress Lanier looked relieved. She said that though she was not a Jew herself, she had some sympathy for these persecuted people. And her family owed a great deal to the Tedeschis.'

'What happened? I mean, what led up to Sarah vanishing?'

'It seems that some time ago, her father, Dr Jacob Tedeschi, was summoned to the palace of the Montemoro family. They are a very grand family in Venice. He had not been there before, though he is well known in the city as a skilled doctor. He took Sarah with him as his nurse.'

'Who was the patient?' said Ned breathlessly.

She shrugged. 'I can't remember exactly. Some relation of the Countess of Montemoro. Anyway, Sarah was left alone with the patient for a short while . . .'

'And the patient died and they blamed Sarah?'

'No, no. That's what's so strange. The patient recovered. But the next day the Countess accused Sarah of casting a spell against the Count.'

'Against the *Count*?'

'The Countess says the girl put the evil eye on him. She says he hasn't been the same since Sarah was there.'

Ned couldn't help snorting. 'The evil eye! What superstitious rubbish!'

'That's what Father said. He asked if Sarah Tedeschi was pretty.'

'Oh ho,' said Ned.

'Oh ho yes,' said Celia, dimpling. 'Apparently the Tedeschi girl *is* very pretty. And the Countess is a very jealous and difficult woman. Mistress Lanier thinks the Countess suspects her husband has fallen in love with the girl. Accusing her of witchcraft is one way of destroying her.'

'But you said Sarah was missing, not arrested.'

'Yes. That's odd too. Mistress Lanier says that the Countess has not made an official accusation. Not yet, anyhow. She sent a letter to the Tedeschis' house informing them she was going to bring a suit against them. And that night Sarah vanished, leaving her father a note. It said she believed she was the victim of a conspiracy and wanted to find proof.'

'Oh, my sweet lord,' said Ned weakly. *This is a knotty drama like something out of one of the Globe plays,* he thought. 'What did the father do?'

'Mistress Lanier said that Dr Tedeschi tried to find her, but had exhausted all avenues of investigation. One thing he did find out was that Sarah had help from outside the Ghetto to escape—the Ghetto's where Jews live, in Venice—so it follows that her helper must be a

Christian. And a Jew making enquiries about a Christian can run into trouble. Besides, the Montemoros are looking for Sarah too and they have tentacles everywhere in Venice. People are afraid of them. Sarah's father didn't know who else to turn to but the daughter of his old friend.'

'What's he going to think when he finds out she's giving the commission to a total stranger?'

'Mistress Lanier will give him a letter of introduction.'

'Did your father agree to this plan?'

'He did. He said it was a noble venture and he would do it.'

'But what if Sarah's found before we get there? It's a long way to Venice,' said Ned reasonably, though his heart thumped with excitement.

'That's what Father said,' said Celia. 'But Mistress Lanier said we would just have to play it by ear.'

'*We?*'

'You don't think I'm going to let Father do all the investigating, do you?' said Celia pertly. 'He's got enough on his plate with the piracy business. I'm a girl. It's easier for me to go around asking around about another girl. And I had those Italian lessons all last year. My teacher said I was very fluent. Even Father agreed about that.'

Celia's father, who thought his own Italian was a bit rusty, had engaged an old Italian philosopher called

Dr Rizzardo to teach her. Rizzardo had said Celia had a real ear for languages. Indeed, he had gushed, she spoke his language now almost as well as a native Italian. 'So I proposed myself to Mistress Lanier,' Celia finished.

'Really! You didn't!' Ned was filled with a mixture of annoyance and admiration. 'Surely your father won't agree.'

'Father will do what I want,' said Celia airily. 'You'll see.'

Yes, thought Ned, *she's right. She's always right. She's got her widowed father wound around her little finger. She's the apple of his eye. And mine . . .* 'I'll help you,' he said firmly.

Celia raised her eyebrows. 'Well, I suppose you could' was all she said.

FORTUNE'S CARDS

Two weeks passed. They took passage on a Venice-bound ship belonging to one of Master Ashby's fellow merchants. The first couple of days were sheer seasick misery for Ned, Mistress Quickly, and Master Ashby. Not so Celia, fresh as a daisy and bright as a sunbeam. She soon had all the hardened sailors eating out of her hand, as well as the other two passengers, a French father and son named Jacques and Henri d'Arcy. Wealthy merchants with business ties to England, the pair spoke good English. And like the Ashbys and Ned, they were bound for Venice. For Jacques d'Arcy's late wife had been Venetian and they still owned a house there.

They went out of their way to be pleasant and friendly, but Ned couldn't stand them. Chiefly, that was because Henri d'Arcy seemed very taken with Celia and spent nearly all his time at her side. To make matters worse, Mistress Quickly, who was chaperoning Celia, approved of Henri—and enjoyed his father's company. There was nothing Ned could do about any of it. What was more, he was stuck in Master Ashby's cabin much of the time, going over accounts and writing letters.

Smouldering with resentment, he watched helplessly as Henri joked and laughed and taught bits of French to Celia and her aunt. What a silver-tongued fop the Frenchman was! Fair-haired, dark-eyed, slim and strong, he was always immaculately dressed and groomed, his pomade smelled good, everything about him breathed wealth, ease, worldliness. At nineteen, he was also a year older than Ned and two years older than Celia, but he seemed a good deal more mature and miles more sophisticated than either of them. Ned hated him with all his heart.

But there was nothing he could say or do. He was just a lowly clerk, at the beck and call of his employer, with an uncertain future and dreams of being a writer, while Henri was a wealthy merchant's son, whose actual future shone like solid gold. *With* solid gold. Piles and piles of gold. Besides, the older Monsieur d'Arcy and

Master Ashby got on famously as well, swapping stories about London, Paris, Venice. Ned's employer, who had once observed that no Frenchman could be trusted, had unbent so far as to declare to his clerk that the d'Arcys were sterling fellows and that he'd go into business with them in the twinkling of an eye. There could be no finer compliment from Matthew Ashby. Mind you, thought Ned, he didn't take the French merchant completely into his confidence—didn't tell him about either the piracy investigation or the Tedeschi case. But then Master Ashby was nothing if not prudent about these sorts of things. It was one of the reasons he had been delegated to go to Venice.

Celia herself seemed to have forgotten about her enthusiasm for investigating Sarah's disappearance. She seemed much more interested in investigating Henri d'Arcy's company, thought Ned sourly. Unhappily, the French fop also had a rather nice line in conversation; the sparkling, witty words Ned so wished he could make his own seemed to just flow effortlessly from Henri's elegant lips. Ned grew glummer and glummer. Celia got crosser and crosser with him. And he could do nothing to remedy the situation. . . .

And then, one day, just a couple of days from Venice, the storm broke. Ned came out of his master's cabin, having finished the morning's work, and went for a breath of air on deck. Neither Celia nor her aunt were to be seen, or Jacques d'Arcy, but Henri was there, leaning on the rail, staring into the water. Ned had a sudden strong urge to push him in. Then a pressing need to get away. He was about to slip off in the opposite direction when the young Frenchman turned and saw him. He smiled.

'*Bonjour!* It is a fine morning, is it not?'

It was indeed. Fine as a day at sea can be. Blue silk sky, lacy little clouds, a light breeze, the calm sea sparkling like jewelled brocade. A day fit for poetry, if Ned had been so inclined. But not that day; not that moment. He growled, 'Fine for those who don't have to work, yes.'

Henri's eyebrows shot up. 'And of whom do you speak, my friend?'

His polite, almost insultingly polite, tone made Ned see red. 'I am not your friend. And you bloody well know what I'm talking about.'

Henri's face closed. 'I do not.'

'You . . . you French . . . you . . . you . . .' The words choked in his throat. He couldn't bring them out.

'Master Fletcher,' said Henri very coldly. 'Beware.'

'What do you mean by that?' rumbled Ned.

'I think you know,' said Henri, shrugging.

'No. I do not. State it in plain words, sir,' said Ned, incensed by the other's tone.

'For sweet Jesus' sake . . . ,' sighed Henri. 'Stop being so belligerent. I am not your enemy. If I make myself amusing to Mademoiselle Celia and Madame Quickly, what of it? Is there a law against such a thing? You would do best to follow my lead, if you wish to win her heart. For you do, do you not, my friend?'

'I am not your friend,' said Ned between gritted teeth.

'No. You are your own worst enemy,' said Henri d'Arcy wearily. 'And this foul humour will not avail you in the least with Mademoiselle Celia.'

'How dare you,' hissed Ned. 'You keep out of my affairs. Keep right out, if you know what's good for you.'

Henri d'Arcy looked Ned up and down. With a scornful look he said, 'You make threats to me! But you are a nobody—I am a d'Arcy. What can you possibly do to me?'

Ned's hand leaped to his sword. A wild, hot anger, stronger and more violent than anything he'd ever felt in his life, spewed into his throat. 'I can fight you,' he challenged d'Arcy.

Henri laughed. 'Here?' He waved around him. 'On the ship? Are you mad? You will be put in chains at once if you try.'

'Very well, then. Not here,' said Ned, dropping his hand. 'I will fight you in Venice. And I'm warning you—in the meantime stay away from her!' The rash words came out of him fast, like hot stones thrown out of a smouldering volcano that had finally erupted. He hardly recognized that it was himself saying them.

Henri d'Arcy's eyebrows lifted. 'Fine words. But deeds cost more.'

Ned went deathly pale. But all he said was, 'Well, *will* you fight me in Venice?'

'You fool,' said Henri d'Arcy. 'You don't know what you're doing. I am reckoned to be one of the finest swordsmen in Paris.'

'I am not afraid of you,' growled Ned, though his heart beat fast and his scalp prickled. 'Set a date and a place.'

Henri d'Arcy's eyes narrowed. 'Very well, then. The day after we arrive, meet me at the stroke of midnight, at the corner of the Bosco Alley. It runs off Bosco Street, two streets back from the Cannaregio canal. You can't miss it. And it's quiet. The guards don't come near it. Come alone. Agreed?'

'Agreed,' said Ned coldly, and stalked away, shaking a little, the blood pounding in his head. The die was well and truly cast now, Fortune's cards on the table. And for that he was glad.

But after the first heady excitement of the challenge had worn off, he began to feel scared. Not scared of the actual fighting. Last year he'd had lessons in swordsmanship from an old friend of Master Ashby's, a man who'd once been a soldier. Master Ashby said every young man should know how to use a sword. And strangely, despite his general clumsiness and dreaminess, Ned had been good at it. His teacher had even praised him: said he could make a living at it, if he'd had a mind to it. . . . Not that he had. Ned didn't at all fancy the footloose life of a soldier, always scrounging for money, or the dangerous one of the paid bodyguard or hired sword, unable to maintain any kind of family life or home.

He could hardly believe he'd actually called a duel. He usually only dreamed of adventure and excitement and danger. Now the real thing had come to him. What was more, he had *made* it come to him. And now he had cold feet! But there was no way he could call off the duel. He would look like a dishonourable coward. No. He would fight hard, and fight to win, and trust to God he wouldn't be killed or badly wounded.

But if he *did* win, it would be because he'd killed or badly hurt Henri. What would happen then? What would Jacques d'Arcy do? The merchant was friendly, but Henri was clearly the apple of his eye, and if anything happened to him he would want the perpetrator punished. And he had influence in Venice. Things could get very sticky indeed. No, at all costs, he must avoid involving Celia or Master Ashby or Mistress Quickly. They must not know a thing. It would be much safer for them that way.

THAT WAY MADNESS LIES

Venice! Venice at last! Though he'd seen it in the painting and onstage, nothing had really prepared Ned for the reality of the golden city. Everything was so much bigger, so much more awesome and magnificent than he'd imagined: the lagoon no gentle pond, but huge, with the powerful salty surge of the sea in it; the blue and gold of St Mark's Basilica, with its vast domes and arches and tall red bell-tower; the pink marble and filigree of the Ducal Palace; the elegant silhouettes of palaces, crowded on the splendid sweep of the Grand

Canal; the busy fleets of gondolas plying the waters, the colourful crowds of people thronging the city . . .

It was a city that might in some lights look like the set for a vast play. And yet it was living, breathing, heaving with noise and colour and possibility. It daunted and excited Ned in almost equal measure. Here was the life of his dreams, the place where anything might happen. *Anything*.

A voice behind him made him start. 'Well, Ned? What do you make of Venice?' He turned. It was Jacques d'Arcy.

'Beautiful, sir! Exciting . . . fantastic . . .'

'All those things and more. *Enchanted*. A mixture of beauty and menace,' said the elder d'Arcy gravely. 'Never forget that, Ned, and you'll get on well here. I've always thought of Venice as a woman,' he went on. 'One of those half-women from legend—beautiful woman to the waist, serpent below. I think that should be her symbol—not the lion.'

Ned shivered. 'That's a horrid thought, sir.'

'Oh, not really,' said the merchant, smiling. 'It's exciting. Intriguing. Just so long as you know to beware. Not to blunder into situations you don't understand.' He looked at Ned. 'Do you understand?'

Ned swallowed. Surely Jacques d'Arcy didn't know about the duel? No, it must be a more general warning. He said, 'I . . . I understand, sir. I'll be careful.'

'That's a sensible resolution, Ned,' said Master Ashby, bustling up to them with his sister and daughter close behind him. 'Avoid the fleshpots of Venice, there's a good lad.'

'Of course, sir,' said Ned, going scarlet, because Celia had heard and was smiling as though it were very funny. Fleshpots indeed! As if he were some kind of young lout, some randy rowdy who couldn't be trusted!

Matthew Ashby ignored his embarassment. He'd spotted someone in the crowd thronging the quay. 'Orlando! My God, look at him. He's hardly changed at all. He must be using some of his own magic potions, that Venetian reprobate!' He turned to the French merchant, all smiles. 'Well, Monsieur d'Arcy, we must say goodbye—and thank you for your company on the ship. It was most pleasant.'

'It was for us too,' said Jacques d'Arcy, smiling, 'and I for one am determined that this is not "goodbye," but merely "till we meet again," and very soon. Perhaps after you have settled—say, in three days' time—you might do us the honour of dining with us? Shall we say six o'clock? I'll send some post-chaises round for you. I know where your friend Dr Leone's house is—he is one of the most famous alchemists in Venice. I have met him myself a few times. Do give him my regards.'

As Master Ashby accepted the invitation and exchanged pleasantries with the French merchant, Ned caught Henri's eye. He read the same question in his enemy's eyes. Which one of them would be alive—or in a fit state—to attend the dinner?

Dr Orlando Leone did not at all fit the popular picture of an alchemist, which tended to be bespectacled, stooped, elderly, absentminded, and wild-eyed. Although he was about Matthew Ashby's age, Leone looked years younger: he was a handsome giant of a man, with a mane of golden hair, broad shoulders under fur-trimmed black robes, and a booming voice.

He was unusual amongst alchemists too, because his family had been quite poor. But a quick intelligence and charm, a talent for money, and a lust for learning had soon seen Orlando Leone improve his position. By the time Matthew Ashby had met him he was already a considerable figure in the city, with a tidy fortune he'd made in partnership with a shipping merchant, and a growing reputation as a talented alchemist—a reputation that had risen spectacularly since then. He had written several books about his science, books that sold well even in England.

'Well, well, and what a most tremendous pleasure!' boomed Dr Leone. His English was good, if rather heavily accented, his voice deep and resonant. 'When I received your letter, my dear Mateo,' he went on, using the Italian form of Matthew's name, 'I pressed it to my bosom, so happy was I that we would meet again after so many years!' He suited the action to the word by clasping Matthew Ashby in a great bear hug from which the stout little merchant emerged breathless and pink-cheeked.

'It's very good to see you too, Orlando,' he managed to gasp. 'May I present my sister, Mistress Bess Quickly, and my daughter, Celia.'

Orlando Leone bowed low over their hands. 'Charmed! Enchanted! Overwhelmed! Dear ladies, welcome with all my heart to Venice. I will endeavour to do everything in my power to make your stay happy and pleasurable.'

'Why, thank you, sir,' said Bess Quickly, a little flustered. As for Celia, she smiled radiantly and said she already loved Venice, just on sight, and she already knew it was all going to be just wonderful.

Ned stood around, feeling superfluous. He had been introduced in a cursory manner as 'Ned Fletcher, my clerk and a good lad,' but Dr Leone hadn't paid him much attention. Not surprising. Clerks didn't figure much in the orbit of a famous alchemist—any more than they were noticed, he thought bitterly, when handsome, wealthy merchants' sons hove into the horizon of pretty young girls with an eye to the future.

He was jerked from his unpleasant thoughts by something Dr Leone was saying. 'Dear ladies, as my house is rather small and devoid of feminine comforts, and as I know Mateo and young Fletcher here will have a good deal of tiresome business to attend to, I have taken the liberty of arranging a set of fine quarters for you in a house a short distance away from mine. It's a beautiful house belonging to one of my very good patrons, Ludovico Marinetti, and it is fully provided with servants. I can even arrange for guides to show you the city. I trust that might be to your satisfaction?' he went on, bowing to Celia and Mistress Quickly.

'Oh yes, that will be just fine,' fluttered Mistress Quickly.

'So very thoughtful of you.' Celia smiled.

But Ned was horribly dismayed. Not only would he have 'all that tiresome business' to attend to, but he wouldn't even be in the same house as Celia! And tomorrow he might be lying dead in some Venetian alley, or on the run for his life. . . . Oh, things were announcing themselves just fine and wonderful, weren't they! He didn't think he was so fond of adventure—no, not any more! Things would have been better if they'd stayed in London.

But Ned's gloomy thoughts faded as they set off through the city, the porters carrying their luggage. Away from the square, the crowds were thinner, but it was still fairly busy—only with foot and water traffic, though: one of the things Ned noticed straight away was the complete absence of horses and horse-drawn vehicles. The canals, big and little, crisscrossed the place, and the little footways beside them were far too narrow, the paving too slippery, for horses. So people walked, or rode in boats, or in post-chaises on the shoulders of porters. Goods were ferried on the water and carried by men up the steps of landing-stages directly into houses fronting onto the canals.

He was all eyes and ears now as they walked deeper into the heart of the city, over little bridges, past churches and fountains and small, paved squares. The spell of the city was already working its way into him little by little, and as he walked along, dreamily hanging back behind the others, looking all around him, imagining stories around people he glimpsed, he felt himself becoming calmer. Things would work out, he told himself hopefully. Now he was here, in magical Venice, things would somehow solve themselves. He'd beat Henri without killing or really hurting him, he'd help Master Ashby with the piracy investigations, and perhaps he might solve the mystery of Sarah Tedeschi's disappearance single-handed and earn the plaudits of everyone . . . and win Celia's heart and hand, through his brave and clever actions. . . .

Deep in his dreams, he had lingered behind the others. Now he suddenly looked up and saw that they had vanished. He was in a square from which several streets radiated. Which one had they taken? He had no idea. Then a thought jumped into his mind. The alchemist was famous. So he would ask the way to Dr Leone's house. Someone was bound to know.

He looked around for help, but there was no one to be seen except for a ragged white-haired figure huddled in the doorway of a church. A beggar of some sort. Well, beggars might be rascals, but they usually knew their way around fairly well. He went over to the beggar, dropped a coin in front of him, and tapped him on the shoulder.

'Er . . . *scusi*—how do you say "I'm looking for a house"? . . . Oh yes, that's right, *ho cercare casa,*' he floundered, trying to remember the scraps of Italian he'd learned from the phrase-book Celia had brought with her and which he'd studied at odd moments on the ship.

The beggar looked up. His hair might have been white, but he wasn't old. It was hard to tell his true age, though, for he was a wreck of a man, painfully thin, the eyes burning, hollow in the gaunt face. Those eyes searched Ned's. The beggar croaked, 'Help . . .'

Ned goggled at him. 'What? Dear God, you're English!'

'Help . . . ,' said the beggar again. He stared wildly at Ned. 'Lost . . . find . . . help . . .'

'You're lost? Oh, I can't help you; I'm a stranger to Venice and in fact I—'

The beggar snatched with a skinny claw at Ned's sleeve. 'Beatrice—where is Beatrice?'

Ned stared. 'Sorry, my friend. I don't know anyone called Beatrice.'

The beggar shrieked so suddenly Ned nearly jumped out of his skin. 'Why do you mock me?'

'What? I'm not—'

'Devil! Sent from hell to mock me!' screeched the man. Without warning, he leaped for Ned's throat.

Ned yelled, stumbled, tripped, fell. The beggar was on him in an instant.

Ned struggled desperately to fight him off, but the man had the unnatural strength of the raving mad. If someone hadn't come on the scene at that instant and flown to Ned's aid, there was no telling what might have happened. In a trice, the man pulled the beggar off Ned and gave him a blow that sent him reeling back into the doorway, where he crouched with his head in his hands, rocking himself and babbling incoherently.

Ned's rescuer said something to him in Italian, which Ned took to mean 'Are you all right?'

Panting, his heart racing, he nodded gratefully. *'Grazie, signore.'*

'Prego,' said the man, shrugging. You're welcome. He pointed to the beggar. *'Pazzo. Pazzo lunatico,'* he said, tapping his head in the universal gesture that signifies 'crazy.'

'Yes—I mean, *si,*' said Ned.

The man smiled. *'Inglese?'*

'*Si*. I'm English—er, *Inglese*.' He pointed at the beggar.

'He spoke English, but kind of rusty. Do you know who he is?' Ned saw the man had not understood at all. He said carefully, 'I mean—*chi es?*'

The man shook his head, shrugged, and spread his hands, to indicate he didn't know. He sighed. *'Povera creatura.'*

'Poor creature. Yes.' Ned glanced at the madman. Pity flooded through him. How could a person come to this? What torturous experience had taken this man's reason from him and brought him to madness? He'd never know. Sighing, he turned away from the sad sight and back to his rescuer. *'Scusi—signore—ho cercare—casa Dottore Leone. Orlando Leone,'* he said carefully.

The man's face cleared. He said brightly, *'Ah! Dottore Leone!'* He pointed to one of the streets across the square, then made a gesture to indicate a left turn. Then he said slowly and clearly, *'La prima casa a destra.'*

Destra, destra, thought Ned hastily. *I think that's right, isn't it? So I have to turn left on that street and then it'll be the first house on the right. Unless I've made a mistake, of course, and it's left. Well, it'll be one or the other, anyway. And they must be wondering where I've got to.* He nodded and said, *'Si, signore. Molto grazie.'*

'Prego,' said the man with a smile.

'Arrivederci, signore,' said Ned, proud of himself for having managed it.

'Arrivederci,' said the man, raising a hand in farewell as Ned set off at a run across the square.

A Venetian window

Dr Leone's house was tall and narrow and three storeys high, built of plain, thin red bricks. The front of the house gave onto a peaceful backwater of a little canal, with a landing-stage and a boat tied up to it. The back looked out into a pleasant little courtyard and a quiet street.

Inside, the house was spacious and pleasant, and furnished comfortably but sparsely. No fashionable gilt or carved things, but solid tables, chairs, and beds, and a few fine tapestries. On the first floor were three large bedrooms: Ned and Master Ashby would occupy two of these, the third being Dr Leone's own room. On the second floor were small bedrooms for the servants. But the third floor housed Dr Leone's work areas: a large laboratory, kept locked when the alchemist wasn't using it, several storerooms, and a small but well-stocked library. All in all a good, plain, serviceable house.

But the Marinetti house where Celia and Mistress Quickly were to stay was very different. It was much bigger and more imposing, for a start. It boasted several pillars and arches, and its brickwork had been rendered with whitewash to make a background for some magnificent frescoes of classical scenes. Inside, the house was most richly furnished in the fashionable Italian manner: the ceilings elaborately painted with scenes from myth; the floor in the main reception room made of lovely black and white mosaic; a good deal of gilt on the carved furniture; silk hangings; and large, elaborate paintings. The Marinettis were very wealthy merchants, and clearly they believed, unlike Dr Leone, that if you had money, it should hit your visitors right in the eye.

The women were delighted with their new quarters. 'It's like a palace,' said Celia, twirling around the room as Ned brought her luggage in. 'Like a palace—and we're the queens.'

'Don't get too queenly,' said Ned tartly. 'Or your subjects might rebel.'

'Will they?' said Celia, giving him a look from under her lashes that made his heart lurch. Did she know . . . did she know what he felt? She'd never say, would she? She would let him stew. Let him stew, while she teased and twinkled and dimpled.

'What are you looking so fierce about?' said Celia. 'Aren't you happy to be in Venice? I thought you'd love it here. You could use it as a setting for one of those poems you're always scribbling. What do you scribble about, Ned?'

He swallowed. She was looking at him in the usual way: friendly, familiar, laughing. Why should she know what he really felt? He'd never told her. Never shown her. Just acted like a gruff older brother.

'Just things,' he said quietly. 'And yes, of course I'm happy to be in Venice. Aren't you?'

'I'm thrilled,' she said simply, her smile radiant. She went to the window and flung open the shutters. 'Oh, Ned, come and look, do!'

He went over. It was certainly worth looking at. Celia's window gave out onto a view of the canal. It was a beautiful sunny day, and gondolas and other boats plied up and down the waterway, many of them flying colourful flags. The canal was lined on both sides with lovely houses as far as the eye could see. Suddenly feeling light and joyful, Ned looked and looked, thoroughly enjoying the feeling of being at a Venetian window with Celia, watching the world go by.

'It's like a dream,' he said. 'I never imagined I'd be here, one day, looking out at this.'

'Yes,' said Celia. 'Oh, Ned—don't you think it's even better, and more beautiful, than we *could* have imagined?'

He glanced sideways at her, his heart beating fast. 'Yes,' he murmured.

She said in a different tone of voice, 'Ned, I've been thinking about our problem. Sarah Tedeschi, I mean. I think the most likely person to have helped her leave the Ghetto is someone who cares deeply about her and would risk a good deal for her sake—most likely a lover.'

'Dr Tedeschi didn't mention any lover in his letter to Mistress Lanier, did he?' said Ned, his eyes on Celia's face. How lovely she was, he thought, lovely, intelligent, spirited; there was more life in her little finger than in ten thousand Helen of Troys. . . . If only he could say it, and not just write it . . . if only he had the courage.

'Fathers don't always know everything about their daughters,' said Celia, shrugging.

Ned shot a sharp glance at her. Had there been a personal undertone to her words? 'She is a few months over sixteen,' Celia went on. 'And Mistress Lanier said she was very pretty. It is most unlikely that such a girl would want for suitors. Now, she is a Jewish girl. And Dr Tedeschi thinks someone outside the Ghetto must have helped her—therefore, it follows that her lover must be not a fellow Jew, but a Christian.'

'Like Jessica and Lorenzo in *The Merchant of Venice,*' said Ned.

'Who? Oh, not another play. Ned, this is real life. The real world. Don't keep harping on about made-up things. Now, listen. I believe we should try to discover who her lover may be. I do not think it is the kind of thing Father would be very good at, so it's up to me—and you, of course, I'd never do it without you,' she added hastily, seeing Ned's expression.

'How do you think we should do it?' he said carefully.

'If Sarah fled the Ghetto with the help of a Christian, I think it must be someone who either has business in the Ghetto or lives near it. He must be someone who has contact with the Jews. Ergo, we must go to the Christian areas nearest the Ghetto and make some discreet enquiries.'

'You've worked it all out, haven't you?' said Ned.

'I've been thinking about it a bit, that's all,' she said pertly. 'Father told me that the Ghetto is actually on a small island in the heart of the district of Cannaregio. So I think that we should be looking around there.'

Ned gave a little gasp, remembering the rendezvous with Henri. 'Did you say Cannaregio?' he said faintly.

'What's the matter?' said Celia sharply.

He shook his head and stammered, 'No . . . nothing.

Just something . . . er, something I heard. It . . . er . . . I heard it was a rather tough sort of area. A bit . . . er . . . dangerous. Too dangerous for a young woman and . . .' He trailed off.

She glared at him. 'Who told you that?'

'Just . . . someone . . . someone I was speaking to, just before. I met them on the way here. Celia, guess what—I managed to speak some Italian, so I can't be as tin-eared as all that! I was able to string quite a few words together. You see, I—'

'Yes, yes, tell me about it later,' said Celia impatiently. 'Anyway, you need not worry about me. I'm not going as a girl—but a boy.'

'What!' said Ned, diverted from his story. 'You can't do that! Your father—'

'If you say anything to him I'll never speak to you again, Ned Fletcher!' cried Celia, fire in her eyes. 'And that's God's truth! Never ever!'

'No, no, I won't say anything,' he stammered desperately, 'of course I won't, but Celia, how will you—'

'Wait and see,' she said, tossing her head. 'Meet me outside this house, tomorrow morning, after Father's left.'

'Where's he going?' said Ned, staring.

'To the Ghetto, to meet Dr Tedeschi. He told me he would be going in the early morning. After that he's going to meet with Salerio's son.'

'With who?' said Ned, confused.

She snorted impatiently. 'Don't you remember? Salerio was the Venetian agent for Father's group. The one who was murdered. His son has taken over the business. Father thinks he may know something.'

Ned nodded. 'Oh. Right.' Then something else she'd said struck him. 'But wait—you said he was going to the Ghetto with Dr Leone!'

'Yes. So?'

'He must have told the doctor what was going on, then.'

'Of course. He said Dr Leone was completely trustworthy. What's more, the doctor knows the Ghetto, as he's interested in old Hebrew books or something. . . . Anyway, listen, Ned. I'll be watching from the window to see when he leaves for the Ghetto. Give him a few minutes' head start and then come over. I'll wait for you downstairs. Mistress Quickly might want to come, of course, but I'll try to stall her. If she does, we'll find a way to lose her somewhere. Agreed?'

'Agreed,' said Ned, staring at Celia. *She really is enjoying this,* he thought. *She fancies herself very much as general of our little campaign. And I'm to be her foot-soldier. . . . Never mind, I'll show her. I'll show her how brave and resourceful I am too. . . .*

'Oh, and see if Dr Leone has a map of the city somewhere, and bring it with you,' Celia went on, blithely unaware of his train of thought. 'Now, if you don't mind, I'm really tired and need a rest.'

There was no doubt it was a dismissal—and a pretty firm one at that. There was nothing Ned could do but swallow his pride and retreat from the Marinetti house in as dignified a manner as he could manage.

A STRANGE EXPEDITION

That night, at the simple dinner they all shared at his house, Dr Leone told them a little about the Countess of Montemoro, who had accused Sarah Tedeschi of witchcraft.

The Montemoros were an old Venetian family, he said. Once, they had been very powerful, and Montemoros had sat on the Council of Ten, the ruling body of Venice. But in the lifetime of the previous Count, a violent drunk and gambler, the family had lost both reputation and fortune. They were only rescued from ruin, explained Dr Leone, by the present Count's marriage to Magdalena da Piero, the present Countess. She came from one of the richest families on terra firma, which was what Venetians called the mainland. Magdalena had come with a very large dowry and a hard nose for business. She had soon set about repairing the Montemoro fortunes. These had prospered beyond anything her husband could have dreamed of. Their only child, Isabella, would be a very rich prize for a suitor one day. But to the Countess's fury, the Montemoro family had still not been reinstated into the Council of Ten; her husband, the Count, was reckoned to be a weak and unreliable man. Besides, Venetians were snobs; the Count was thought to have married beneath him, for the da Pieros, though wealthy and influential, were not from the old Venetian families listed in the city aristocracy's Golden Book.

'She's a piece of work,' said Dr Leone with feeling. 'I call her "the she-wolf"—the emblem of the Montemoros features a wolf's head—and she no doubt calls me something just as unflattering.' It turned out they had clashed over the fact she disapproved of alchemy, calling it 'mere sorcery and charlatanism.' She had even tried to influence the Duke to issue a banning order against alchemists. 'But fortunately, I, unlike her, have the ear of the Duke,' he went on, 'and that sour gorgon was sent packing with a flea in her ear! She's a nasty piece to cross, though, if you have no influence. She's rich as Midas these days, what's more, for all her ventures prosper and her ships come home safely laden with goods.'

'Lucky Countess,' said Matthew Ashby glumly. 'That's not the case for us lesser mortals, caught in the grip of ruthless pirates.'

'I'm sure the pirates, cruel as they are, would be far too frightened of the Countess's reputation to risk getting on her bad side,' said Dr Leone, smiling rather grimly. 'They'd bite off more than they can chew, attacking a Montemoro ship. She'd pursue anyone who did her wrong to the ends of the earth, of that I am sure. Well! I wouldn't give a fig for this Tedeschi girl's chances, if she's caught by the Montemoro she-wolf, so we must try and stop it happening.'

The next day dawned grey and drizzly. Master Ashby and Dr Leone went off early in the morning as planned, but in a covered post-chaise rather than on foot. Ned, watching at the window, waited till the post-chaise had vanished from sight before going over to the Marinetti house. But Celia wasn't outside yet. He waited, stamping his feet to try and keep warm. He took a look up and down the street. Not a soul was stirring. He wouldn't mind being inside with Celia, curled up in front of a nice warm fire in her room, and . . .

Stop it, he told himself sternly. *You must tread carefully. You must not annoy her. You must not rush things.*

You must not frighten her away. Remember, there's Henri still lurking around and . . . But the thought unfortunately started another one. What would happen that night? Would he see the next day's dawn? Or would he be lying in his own blood in some dark alley and—

'Psst,' Celia's voice said, behind him.

He started, turned and stared, amazed. Celia's blue eyes smiled at him from a dirty face; her hair had been rubbed with cinders to dull its colour and then expertly pinned up and shoved under a large, shabby velvet cap. The doublet and hose she was wearing were stained and crumpled, and over them she wore a shapeless dark cloak.

'What's the matter, Ned? You look like you've seen a ghost!'

Ned found his voice. 'Where *did* you get those dreadful clothes?'

'Found them in the servants' quarters,' she said defiantly.

'You mean you took them! Oh, Celia, what will your father do if he finds out?'

'He won't,' she said firmly. 'Will he?' she added, crossing her arms and glaring at him.

'No . . . no . . . I mean, not from me. But someone might talk. The servants . . .'

'They didn't see me.'

'And your aunt?'

'She was snoring heartily when I left. I don't think

she'll wake before midday. You know she loves her sleep. We'll be back before she knows I've even stirred.'

'If you say so,' he said quietly. In her shabby clothes and bizarre disguise Celia suddenly looked both stranger and more approachable. She didn't look like a rich merchant's only daughter any more, but a street child with fewer prospects even than a lowly clerk. One thing was, she didn't look at all like a boy to him—she never could—but to someone who didn't know her, she might well pass muster. His heart was beating fast. Going on this strange expedition with her was something he would not have missed for the world.

'Now, Ned,' said Celia brightly, 'did you find a map?'

Smiling, Ned fished in his clothes. 'Yes. Here it is. I've already looked at where we should go. See, here? If we go back to that little square up there, and then turn here and . . .'

Cannaregio is one of Venice's oldest districts and the most northerly. It stretches in an arc bounded on one side by the Grand Canal and the other by quays that look out towards the islands in the lagoon. A mixture of the grand and the shabby, its alleys and canals are always busy, and that day, despite the weather and the early hour, it was already a bustle of market colour and activity.

Here, in the heart of Cannaregio, the Ghetto was very close. Because Jews were forbidden to live anywhere but on the isle, they had to build up into the air rather than sideways, so their buildings were very tall, up to six floors—the tallest buildings Ned and Celia had ever seen.

The gates that led across the two bridges into the Ghetto had been unlocked at sunrise, and Jews in their regulation red cloaks and yellow hats mingled in the busy market scene. Most of them were men or boys, but there were a few women amongst them, mostly matrons of a certain age, and once a pretty young girl, walking rapidly behind her parents, head down.

'Ned, don't stare,' hissed Celia in his ear.

Ned had not meant to be rude. But in London, despite Master Ashby's liberal attitude, he had rarely come into contact with Jews, and certainly not so many or so varied in looks as the Venetian Jews. Some were dark as Moors, others fair as Germans, others still little different from the other Venetians who milled and bustled amongst them—except for those distinctive cloaks and hats. Here, Jews were officially protected by the state and the Ghetto was guarded at night by Venetian watchmen. But even if malefactors could not invade the Ghetto at night, its inhabitants could not leave either. And during the day, when they could circulate freely, they were required to wear the yellow hat and the red cloak. *It must be strange, to live like that,* Ned thought suddenly. *To be for ever marked.*

'Look.' Celia dug him in the ribs. A wolfishly handsome young man in cheap finery had waylaid the family of the pretty young girl. He was talking rapidly to the father, while his eyes kept darting to the girl. She kept her eyes down, but there was a tension about her, like a deer poised for flight, that made it clear she was uncomfortably aware of the young man's scrutiny.

The young man stopped talking. He put a hand on the shoulder of the older man, who visibly stiffened, then gave a faint smile. He nodded in farewell, gathered up his family, and walked on swiftly. The girl didn't look back. Not once. But the young man stood there for an instant, watching them go.

'I'm going to talk to him,' said Celia, and before Ned could react, she was off, elbowing her way through the crowd to where the young man stood. Ned hurried after her.

'But what are you going to say to him?' he hissed. 'You can't just ask him if he's seen Sarah Tedeschi! Anyway, why should he?'

'Just wait and see,' said Celia infuriatingly. '*Signore,*' she said as they reached the young man. '*Signore, per favore . . .*' She held out a hand on which, to Ned's astonishment, reposed a silver coin. He hadn't even seen her palm it out of her purse. He hadn't known she was capable of such a thing. Was there to be no end to Celia's surprises?

The young man stared at her. Then Celia unleashed a torrent of seemingly fluent Italian, hardly any of which Ned could understand, but which he took to mean was some sort of explanation that she had seen him drop that silver coin just a little distance away and was keen to give it back to him. The young man listened without saying anything, his bright dark eyes resting thoughtfully on Ned. Then he said something to Celia, and she nodded.

'Grazie. Molto grazie,' said the young man slowly, and took the silver coin from Celia's hand. He bit it, obviously suspecting it was some sort of forgery. Satisfied, he looked at them again, this time especially at Ned. *'Grazie,'* he repeated.

'Er . . . *prego,*' Ned answered falteringly, as the thanks seemed to be aimed at him.

The man smiled. *'Straniero?'* Ned understood that. The man was asking if he was a foreigner. He didn't want to be just any sort of foreigner.

'Inglese,' he said a little too loudly.

'Ah,' said the young man. He looked at Celia and said something to her in rapid Italian. She grinned and replied.

'I told him I am your guide and servant,' she hissed to Ned as the young man laughed.

Ned frowned, an odd feeling twisting in his guts. 'That's not funny. Why is he laughing?'

'Because I also told him you were a typical barbarian Englishman, who'd never seen anything like Venice before and liked to gawk at everything.'

'Well, thank you very much,' said Ned indignantly.

Celia didn't answer. She was talking to the young man again. He seemed to be in high good humour—and no wonder, thought Ned sourly, with a silver coin he'd got for nothing in his purse and a chance to laugh at barbarian Englishmen!

They talked for a little while. Every so often the young man would shoot one of those bright, blank gazes at Ned, who tried to ignore him.

At last Celia and the man stopped talking. She turned to Ned. 'Time to go. Pretend to get annoyed with me or something, so we can just go, or I think he might hover around us for a while.'

'No wonder, as you've been handing out money for nothing,' said Ned crossly.

'You'll see it's not for nothing. But he's getting a bit nosy now, so I think we should go.'

'What am I supposed to say?' growled Ned. He looked at her, then at the man, watching them with narrowed eyes, and snapped, 'Right. Now, my fine fellow, it's time to stop chattering like this. We have work to do!' And he flapped a hand at Celia. 'Come on, boy! I weary of being kept waiting while you gossip like an old woman!'

The man said something to Celia. She shrugged and fluttered a hand regretfully, making it clear she had to leave with her supposed employer. *'Scusi, signore. Arrivederci.'*

'Arrivederci, l'amico,' said the young man, and Ned could feel the bright eyes boring into his back as they made their way quickly through the crowd.

They walked on rapidly till they had left most of the

crowd behind. They were in a quiet street by a little backwater when Ned stopped. 'Celia, that was quite some performance.'

'Did you think so? Good. They say only men and boys can go onstage. Do you think I would have made a good actor?'

'Celia!' said Ned, scandalized.

She laughed in his face. 'Don't worry. I have no intention of becoming one. Plays bore me. I want real life. That was real life, wasn't it, Ned?'

'It certainly was,' he said wryly, suddenly so badly wanting to kiss her that he had to keep his arms stiffly by his side. In his bossiest big-brother voice, he said, 'Now, Celia, you have to tell me what he said, and whether it was worth that silver coin or not.'

She grinned. 'Well, I said to him that you, heathen Englishman that you are—'

'Celia! Heathen Englishman indeed! I'm no pagan!'

'I know you're not, but to a Catholic, like Italians are, Protestants are little better than heathens. I had to be in character, Ned.'

'Oh. The cheek of those Papists! Right. Then what?'

'I said that you were fascinated by the Ghetto, and particularly Jewish girls.'

'Celia!' protested Ned, shocked.

'Shh. Listen. He said then that Jews were scum, but that their women were mighty beautiful. I said you wanted to know if there was any way of meeting one, in secret. He laughed and said it was not easy, but it could be done. He had seduced dozens himself. I don't believe him for an instant, mind you. He's one of those dirty talkers. I doubt any Jewish girl has even given him the time of day. But, more to our purpose, he also said that though the girls are usually protected by their families, there are ways you might meet them. People come to the Ghetto to work—builders, for instance, carpenters, painters, and such. Jews aren't allowed to build themselves, so they have to bring in tradesmen from outside when they need to build anything, or add to it. Then there's moneylending—he's borrowed money himself. That Jew he spoke to in the street, with his family—that's the moneylender he used. He says he'd love to get close to the daughter, but has not been able to.'

'He looked like a villain to me,' said Ned warmly. 'I think the moneylender would be wise to keep him well away from his daughter.'

'I am sure he knows that,' said Celia drily. 'Anyway, you see. It can be done.'

'Yes,' said Ned. 'That is all very well, but does it get us any closer to the person who helped Sarah? Did you enquire about her?'

'Of course not,' said Celia. 'That would have been far too dangerous.'

'He did not look like a very savoury character,' agreed Ned. 'What are we going to do now?'

'I suppose we should try somewhere else,' said Celia a little doubtfully.

'What about in the Ghetto itself?' said Ned.

'Father and Dr Leone might still be there—they might see us.'

'Well, what of it? We're doing nothing wrong. . . . Oh, of course,' he added as he saw Celia's expression, 'you don't want him to see you like that!' He grinned. 'It's true you look thoroughly disreputable. You easily pass muster as a disgusting Venetian urchin, and no trace of Master Ashby's charming daughter at all. Enough to give my poor employer nightmares!'

Celia blushed and looked away for a moment. 'Perhaps you're right,' she said defiantly. 'We should go to the Ghetto. Better have a different story there, though.' She eyed Ned.

'If you think I'm going to try and pass as some flighty, empty-purse Englishman who needs a loan, you can think again! We can go on some other pretext. Like . . . well . . .' He smiled at her. 'Like I'm just one of those heathen Englishmen who wants to come and gawk at the Ghetto. I'm sure there must be people who come to do just that.'

'I'm sure there are. But nobody will want to talk to you then,' said Celia.

'So what? I can't talk to them. You can do the talking.' He added drily, 'You seem to be good at it. Very good at it.'

Celia shrugged. 'They won't talk much to me either, I wager. It's likely they padlock their tongues when a stranger's about.'

'We might as well try, seeing as we're so close,' said Ned.

They set off, walking rapidly along the side of the canal towards the bridge which led to the Ghetto. Suddenly, Ned gave a little exclamation. 'Oh, no! He's coming this way. . . . Quick, Celia . . .' And he drew her into the shadow of a doorway.

She whispered, 'Is it Father?'

'Shh. No. Wait.' He peered out carefully. 'Good. He's heading in the opposite direction. We can go.'

Celia said, 'What are you talking about?' Her eyes scanned the crowd. Ned pointed and she saw, at some distance, shambling wearily away from them, a twisted wreck of a man with long, tangled white hair. 'Ned, who is that?'

'A crazy man I ran into yesterday—I think he's an Englishman,' said Ned. Rapidly, he told her the story.

Her eyes widened. She put a hand on his arm. She said, 'Oh, Ned, you could have been really hurt!'

'I wasn't,' said Ned, warmed by the expression in her eyes and by her touch. 'But it was horrible, still. Horrible—and sad. That expression on his face . . . the way he called me devil . . . as if he hated me from the bottom of his soul! And yet he didn't know what he was saying. . . . Poor creature.' He sighed. 'It seems terrible to think that he's English; I mean, that he's alone and friendless here, and in that state. I wonder what his story is. . . .'

'I don't suppose we'll ever know,' said Celia, recovering her former briskness. 'And we're wasting time talking about it. Come on, let's go to the Ghetto.'

Do we not bleed?

Surrounded on all sides by canals, the Ghetto of Venice was a miniature city within the city. And like any city it had its share of fair and foul. Those tall, thin houses were not all the same. Some looked shabby, unkempt, poor; others boasted balconies, arched windows, and fountains and quite clearly were the dwellings of the better-off. On the bottom floors of some of the houses were little shops, many selling cloth of one sort or another, for the textile trades, along with medicine and moneylending, were the only ones Jews were legally allowed to practise in Venice.

There were quite a few people about, and Celia tried to ask questions, but drew a blank. It was not until they came across a small boy of about six or seven playing knuckle bones by himself on the step of a house that she managed to get any answers. But they were worth waiting for, for the child chattered away to her quite happily—and incomprehensibly, as far as Ned was concerned.

When they moved away, Celia whispered to Ned, 'He knows Dr Tedeschi. The house is in the next street. He says lots of people, all sorts, go to him to be treated.'

'Do you think this lover of Sarah's might be a patient of her father's?'

'Maybe, though usually when it's a Christian patient the doctor will go to them. It would be mostly Jewish patients visiting the doctor in the Ghetto.'

'But you can only tell someone's a Jew if they wear those hats and cloaks,' argued Ned. 'And Sarah can't be doing that right now, or she'd have been spotted long ago. So why couldn't her lover be doing the same thing? He could be a Jew too.'

'Yes, but then they'd *both* have had to get out of the Ghetto at night,' said Celia. 'The guards would have to be bribed—and I'm sure it would be more expensive for two people, and a much more risky enterprise. No, I'm sure her special friend's a Christian. And listen to this,

Ned—the child said he'd heard his parents say Sarah was accused of being too friendly with some young Gentile—that's what they call us Christians.'

'Really?' said Ned excitedly. 'Who was it?'

'He didn't know. It was just hearsay.'

'But Dr Tedeschi didn't say anything about this in his letter to Mistress Lanier.'

'Maybe it was too delicate a matter. Or maybe it only happened after he sent the letter, which was a few weeks ago. What's more, it's taken us two weeks to get here. A good deal might have happened in that time. In fact,' she added, 'we do not even know how things stand right now, until we speak to Father. I think we should get back home. We need to find out what happened at Dr Tedeschi's before we go any further.'

But Master Ashby and Dr Leone had not come back. They did not arrive till lunchtime. And they did not seem to be in a hurry to talk about what had happened at Dr Tedeschi's, though over the pasta and fish and honey-cakes Master Ashby did speak about his meeting with Angelo, the son of the murdered shipping agent, Salerio.

It had not gone very well at all. Angelo, who seemed very frightened, claimed not to know anything about what his father had discovered. He said his father had told him nothing and, furthermore, that all the papers relating to the piracy had mysteriously vanished. He told them that his agency could no longer handle the London merchants' business, that it would be better for everybody if Master Ashby and his colleagues took their business elsewhere.

It was quite clear that someone had got to him.

Under heavy pressure, Angelo admitted that the London merchants were not the only ones to have lost ships, and that his father, on the last day of his life, had found out interesting information from a source in the nearby city of Verona. This was that a small-time Verona crook called Gamboretto, who operated a business buying up stock from bankrupt merchants, might possibly have a connection with the pirates.

'He said Salerio intended to go there and speak to the man, but was killed before he could do so,' said Master Ashby, now. 'We will have to go to Verona to interview Gamboretto, that's clear. But we will have to move very carefully. Orlando's advised me to get the help and protection of the city authorities before I go any further.'

'We don't want you ending up like poor Salerio, knifed to death in some dark alley,' said Dr Leone grimly. 'These people mean business, you know, Mateo.'

Lunch wore on and still nothing was said about the Tedeschi case. Ned couldn't think of a natural way to introduce the subject, and Celia seemed a little distracted. Then, after lunch, Mistress Quickly went off for a nap and Master Ashby declared that he wanted Ned to write a couple of letters for him. Dr Leone proposed that they adjourn to the library, and Celia declared she would come with them. She couldn't wait to see the books in an alchemist's library, she was sure they'd be so interesting. . . . A white lie, of course, thought Ned, for Celia had never shown the slightest interest in any form of science, let alone alchemy. But of course Dr Leone was delighted.

The library was a small, cosy room, packed from ceiling to floor with books. Only in the bookstalls in St Paul's churchyard in London had Ned ever seen anything like this richness of books. He picked some up at random. They were in all sorts of tongues: Latin, Italian, English, French, German, Spanish. There was even one in a script that looked to Ned for all the world like the wanderings of a spider. Dr Leone told him this was Hebrew and the book was about the Kabbalah, the Jewish teachings of mysticism that interested many alchemists. One of his acquaintances in the Ghetto, he said, was a brilliant Kabbalist, a man called Serafin, who was teaching him Hebrew as well as discussing Kabbalistic principles with him. Serafin had come originally from Alexandria, where, he said, there were many great Kabbalists and other mystics and philosophers; and one day, declared Dr Leone, he himself intended to travel there and study for a few years at the feet of the masters.

After a short while browsing the books, Master Ashby remembered what they'd come for—and Ned was seated at the desk, a fresh sheet of parchment before him and a new quill in his hand.

'Now then,' said Ashby, 'you will begin by saying—'

'Father,' interrupted Celia, clearly unable to wait any longer, 'before Ned starts, can you please tell us what happened this morning?'

Ashby looked at her in surprise. 'But I already told you—'

'No, no. At Dr Tedeschi's house.'

'Nothing much happened, my dear. Just a preliminary talk. We went really to make sure the girl hadn't turned up.'

'And had she?'

Ashby shook his head. 'No. But her father had had another note from her, telling him she was safe and that she was trying to find the proof she had spoken of. Nothing that advanced us much.'

'Oh,' said Celia. 'What manner of man is he—the doctor, I mean?'

'Tall and stooped and soft-spoken, with worried eyes and a sad mouth,' said Matthew Ashby. 'His wife's dead years since and he lives with his sister, Rachel.'

'Fine-looking woman, but a bit of a tartar with a sharp tongue on her,' said Dr Leone, smiling faintly. 'She told us off for being a little late and a little desultory. Then she told us about something else, something unexpected, which rather complicates matters.'

Ned and Celia shot a glance at each other.

'Something about his daughter's friend, sir?' blurted out Ned.

Dr Leone said sharply, 'What do you mean?'

'Nothing,' said Celia, but not quickly enough. Dr Leone said even more sharply, 'What have you been up to?'

'No-nothing, sir,' stammered Ned, but Celia turned to her father and said quickly, 'Now, don't be angry, but Ned and I have been doing a bit of investigating ourselves, and we . . .' She explained what they'd worked out and what they'd discovered, while Matthew Ashby listened in stupefaction and Orlando Leone's face darkened.

When she'd finished, the alchemist was the first to speak. 'Of all the reckless things to do!' he snapped. 'There are informers everywhere in Venice, and one must be careful who one talks to. That young man you spoke to so freely, he may have been one. You may have put the Tedeschis, as well as yourselves, in great danger.' He rounded on Ned. 'What sort of idea of yours was it, dragging my friend's daughter into this dangerous escapade?'

'It wasn't his idea,' said Celia tightly, before an astonished Ned could answer. She looked defiantly at the alchemist. 'It was mine. Ned went along with it.'

'Then you should have remonstrated with her, Master Fletcher, and stopped her!'

Ned said quietly, 'I thought it was a good idea too, sir. I still think it was.'

Celia's eyes flashed. 'And we did not breathe the name of Tedeschi to that young man. We are not such fools as you seem to think, Dr Leone.'

'Now, now, my dear,' said Master Ashby uncomfortably, 'I am sure Dr Leone does not think you are fools. Far from it. But really, you were rather naughty, going off on your own like this without asking anyone.'

'I wasn't on my own,' said Celia. 'I was with Ned.' She moved closer to him. 'There was nothing to fear with him there.'

Ned felt as though his insides were turning to water. Sweet, hot water, coursing through his body. His ears burned. He looked at Celia. She looked at him and smiled. His hands shook. He said, 'I would have protected her with my life, sir, if need be.'

There was a little silence, in which everyone in the room looked at Ned with various degrees of surprise. Then Master Ashby said, 'You're a good and honest boy, Ned, and I know you mean what you say, but you do not know Venice—'

'But you didn't take us with you,' broke in Celia. 'And we want to help. Both of us.'

'I can see why you might,' said Dr Leone, obviously making an effort to control his temper. 'And it says much for your spirit that you did. But you might still have thought carefully before leaving a trail a blind man might follow. It's not only that young man who may be a problem. The child may babble about the strangers who asked him questions about the Tedeschis, and it may get back to the wrong ears.'

'But he's in the Ghetto—it'll only be other Jews he speaks to!' exclaimed Ned, feeling light-headed and lighthearted and not at all anxious.

Dr Leone smiled thinly. 'And in your innocence you think all Jews should agree amongst each other and love each other? But they are men like any others, and as prone to the same feelings, noble and ignoble.'

"'If you prick us, do we not bleed?'" quoted Ned drily.

'What?' said Dr Leone, startled.

'A speech by Shylock, the Jewish moneylender. From *The Merchant of Venice*,' said Ned.

Dr Leone looked puzzled.

'By William Shakespeare,' Ned went on.

Dr Leone still looked puzzled.

Master Ashby sighed. 'Never mind all that. You see, my children, things are complicated. It appears Dr Tedeschi has a bitter enemy within his own community, a wealthy textile manufacturer named Solomon Tartuffo, whose son fell in love with Sarah. The Tartuffos sent a matchmaker to formally ask for her hand, but Sarah abominates the son and her father was in no mind to force her. He said he did not like the young man, or his family either, despite their wealth and status in the community. Solomon Tartuffo was furious at what he called a gross insult and ended up by accusing the Tedeschis to the rabbi—that's their priest, if you like—of planning to abandon their religion to snare some Gentile.'

'Why didn't he tell Mistress Lanier about it, then?'

'He says the whole thing blew up *after* he'd sent the letter to her. When we asked him—delicately, of course—if there was any truth in Tartuffo's accusation, both he and his sister said it was sheer wicked nonsense, that they were all faithful Jews.'

'But Jessica gave up her religion for love and turned her back on her father,' said Ned sadly.

Everyone looked at him. Dr Leone's eyes narrowed. But Celia said crossly, 'Oh, don't worry. He's only talking about that blasted play he saw, not real people.'

Dr Leone raised his eyebrows. 'I see. To continue, Dr Tedeschi said that Sarah knew no Gentiles well. The only one she's seen more than once is a young carpenter called Tomas, who has worked with his father on renovations to the house, some months ago.'

'But that's what we thought, Father!' said Celia excitedly. 'We were sure Sarah's helper must be not only a Christian, but her lover, and—'

Matthew Ashby shook his head. 'Dr Tedeschi swore it was all aboveboard. Tomas is married, as is his father, of course.'

'But that doesn't mean—'

Dr Leone shook his head. 'Dr Tedeschi was quite adamant that his daughter would never do such an immoral thing as carry on with a married Gentile. And the young man in question was absolutely correct in his behaviour, at all times. Dr Tedeschi said the family are honest and very well respected, both in Cannaregio and the Ghetto. He says he trusts them.'

'But maybe, even if this Tomas isn't in love with Sarah, perhaps he might have helped her, as a friend?' said Ned.

'We did raise this with the good doctor, but he was certain that was not so. He said he had asked Tomas and his family point-blank, and they swore they knew nothing about it. He believes them.'

'Then how did she get out?'

'He thinks she must simply have bribed one of the guards. It does happen. And she does have a little money of her own.'

'Perhaps one of the guards is in love with her,' suggested Celia hopefully.

Matthew Ashby laughed. 'Perhaps. That will be our next move. Orlando and I will arrange to speak to the guards, discreetly.'

'May we come with you then, Father?'

'We will see,' said Ashby firmly.

'Sir, did you find out if the Countess knows that Sarah's gone?' asked Ned.

'He thinks she must do by now. He's afraid she's got her spies out, looking for her.'

'Perhaps now you understand why I was so harsh with you, Signorina Celia and Master Fletcher,' said

Dr Leone earnestly. 'I'm sorry, but this could be a matter of life and death, and if you make the wrong move, it's not just the Tedeschis in danger, but yourselves too.'

'Could this Tartuffo—this merchant, who hates Dr Tedeschi—could he be in league with the Countess of Montemoro?' asked Celia.

'It's possible, my dear. We just don't know. These are very murky waters we're wading in,' sighed her father. 'And now, Ned and Celia, you will have to give me your word that you will not go off on any more expeditions like this without telling us. We must work together if we're to solve this with the least danger to everybody, do you see?' His eyes glistened anxiously. 'Promise. Both of you.'

'But, Father—'

'Please, Celia.'

Celia looked sulky. 'Oh, very well, Father. I promise.'

'And so do I,' said Ned a little reluctantly.

'Excellent. Excellent,' said Master Ashby, rubbing his hands together. 'Now then, Ned, let's get these letters written. It's important they go off this very day.'

Flying dreams

The letters were duly finished and sent. The rest of the day wore on. Though Ned had feared that 'tiresome business' would fill the afternoon, taking him away from Celia's side, it didn't turn out like that. Dr Leone, who seemed eager to make amends to the two young people for his harshness, took them and his friend Ashby on a tour of his laboratory.

It was a large, airy, light room. In one corner was a small curtained altar, for alchemists started their day's work with prayer and meditation. Animal skeletons and bunches of dried medicinal herbs hung from the ceiling, and on the whitewashed walls strange symbols and colourful figures of birds had been painted: a raven, a swan, a peacock, a pelican, and a phoenix. There were two large tables in the centre of the room, covered in retorts, crucibles, alembics, tripods, crystallization dishes, a couple of human skulls, and other paraphernalia of the alchemist's art. On one of these tables something was distilling: a bubbling liquid of a silvery colour. One wall was lined with shelves, which were filled with vials, bottles, and jars, most of which contained powdered metals and liquids. There were several adjoining rooms: one which housed the furnaces, for the melting and refining of metals, the others where extra supplies and equipment were kept. It was a very fine setup; in fact, said Dr Leone without false modesty, he thought it was one of the most sophisticated and well-equipped laboratories not only in Venice, or even Italy, but in the whole of Europe. 'It's not just how it's set up either,' he explained, 'it's that the work I'm doing is unique. No one else is attempting anything like it.'

Most alchemists spent their lives in the search for the Philosopher's Stone, the magical ingredient that would not only deliver the method by which base metals could be turned into gold, but also produce the Elixir of Life, which would make men immortal. It was while Dr Leone was still working on these traditional questions of alchemy, many years ago, that Master

Ashby had first met him. But now, he had branched out into a different field.

'The practise of alchemy teaches us that in order to free the spirit to perform extraordinary things, we must become as birds,' he explained. 'We must ascend from the first stage, the darkness of the mind, represented by the raven, to the light of the swan, then the multi-coloured realm of the peacock, and through the sacrifice of the pelican to the triumphant rebirth of the phoenix. We are rebirthed through that flight of the spirit. But for me this is not just a spiritual practise. I believe it can be done in body, in fleshy reality.' His eyes shone. 'Have you ever had flying dreams, my friends?'

They nodded.

'Why is it that in dreams we can fly? When we have flying dreams, we feel it in our bodies, our sinews and bones, as if it were in fact real.'

'But, sir, how can we know that's what flying really feels like?' asked Ned. 'We're not birds! I mean, if we've never done it . . .'

'That's just it,' said Dr Leone. 'I believe we have. Through my meditations, I came upon this extraordinary insight: what if dreams of flying are reminders of an earlier time, when we were not yet sinful mortals but closer to God in all things? Not birds, but more like angels. What if alchemy offers some way of recapturing that lost ability, just as finding the Philosopher's Stone and distilling the Elixir of Life could bring us the immortality of angels? It is known that occasionally people have attempted to fly, and so I began studying a few proven instances of it.'

'I've heard it said at home that witches sometimes fly,' said a wide-eyed Ned. 'They smear an ointment on themselves and then they can do it.'

'Fern-seed ointment, reputedly obtained from the fairies,' put in Dr Leone with a faint smile. 'I've heard of that too, young Ned. I've also heard that they call on the Devil to help them. But I believe the whole thing to be a lie, a claim made by witches to make themselves seem cleverer than they really are. No, I'm afraid those silly, deluded women have got nothing to teach me. The instances I have studied were of real cases: for instance, a fellow alchemist by the name of John Damian, who last century made himself a pair of wings and took off from the ramparts of Stirling Castle, in Scotland.'

'What happened?' cried Ned.

'Oh, he just fell and broke his thigh,' said Dr Leone. 'But that was because he was wrong to look at flight in that manner, as if he were Icarus. Another more interesting case was that of the alchemist known as Miracolo, right here in Venice, more than a hundred years ago—'

'My dear Orlando,' broke in Master Ashby. 'I remember you telling me what happened to him. I wish you would not invoke his name so freely.'

'It was a long time ago,' said Dr Leone, 'and people

were much more superstitious then. Poor Miracolo was a man ahead of his time, a martyr to science. He really did learn the secret of flight. You know, like Serafin, the Kabbalist with whom I'm studying, he was from Alexandria. He wasn't a Jew, though. His mother was a Venetian who had gone to Alexandria and stayed; his father was a very wealthy Alexandrian merchant—Greek, I think. Miracolo came to Venice to visit his mother's people and settled in the city for a few years. He was actually seen to take off from the Rialto bridge one moonlit night and fly three times over the city. Without any wings! Or fern-seed ointment either,' he added, winking at Ned. 'Mateo is right—he finished badly. His enemies claimed that Miracolo had made a pact with the Devil and that he was guilty of unspeakable crimes. Because he refused to divulge his secret, he was tried on a charge of sorcery and sentenced to death. But before they could burn him at the stake he killed himself in prison. His secret died with him—his servants, taking fright at his fate, burned all his papers, and his laboratory was razed to the ground. But in my studies and my experiments I think I am beginning to reconstruct the steps he took to reach his goal—human flight without fake wings or other foolish mechanical aids. Isn't that so, Mateo?'

'From what you've told me since we arrived, you've done some very interesting experiments,' said Ashby cautiously, 'but as I told you earlier, my dear friend,

I thought you were straying into rather dangerous territory. Take care, Orlando. We do not want Miracolo's sad fate to befall you.'

'Oh, as I said, people were much more superstitious back then,' said Dr Leone airily. 'Things have changed now.'

'But if the Countess Montemoro has already tried to accuse you of sorcery . . .'

'She was just laughed at. She cannot do anything to me. I'm no powerless Jewish girl,' said Dr Leone tartly, 'or indeed a foreigner like poor Miracolo. Besides, it is not just me who is interested in seeing whether humans can be enabled to fly. There is interest from the very highest reaches of the state.' He paused. 'Imagine if an army could have a squadron of flying fighters? Imagine if spies could wing their way into enemy territory? The state that possessed such a secret could become immensely powerful.'

'Last century, Leonardo da Vinci had the idea of ships of the air, craft that could sail the skies like boats ply the waters,' said Master Ashby.

Dr Leone shrugged. 'Mere fancies, in my opinion. Such heavy, inanimate things could never fly. What is much more likely is that I can unlock the secret that will make us relearn what was once an ancestral ability. I believe it can be done—and in my lifetime.' His eyes shone. 'Imagine, my friends, being able to leave the confines of earth and sail up into the sky! Why, if this works, I'll be remembered as the man who revolutionized the history of our race!'

Celia said brightly, 'Oh, it would be a wonderful, wonderful thing, Dr Leone!'

'But, Orlando, thousands of alchemists have laboured mightily over the years to create the Philosopher's Stone,' said Master Ashby, 'and yet none has succeeded. This is an even more difficult undertaking.'

'What of it?' said Dr Leone carelessly. 'What's worth doing is worth risking for.'

'But, Orlando—'

'Don't worry, Mateo, I'm not risking that much,' said Dr Leone with a smile. 'Not with the backing of my powerful patrons.'

'I don't like it,' said Ned slowly. 'I can see why a person might want to fly, for the sheer joy of it. But the rest, Dr Leone? Flying fighters? Winged spies? It sounds terrible. How could anybody protect themselves against such monsters?'

Dr Leone shook his head with a pitying smile. 'They won't be monsters, boy. They will be humans as we should be—masters of the sky as well as the earth and the sea.'

'Nobody is master of those except God,' said Ned, flushing.

'Of course not—not in that way,' said Dr Leone

smoothly. 'But we were given dominion over the world—were we not?—and so this would all be in God's plan.'

Ned didn't argue any more. What was the use? Dr Leone was much cleverer than he was. And Celia was looking at him as though she thought he was a narrow-minded, blinkered specimen indeed. *And so maybe I am,* he thought miserably. *Maybe I am. She won't miss me when I'm dead.*

Bosco Alley

Suppertime came. Not such nice food this time—Dr Leone had rather mischievously ordered what he said was a Venetian delicacy: fried frogs, sprinkled with cheese. But Ned was so worried about time ticking on towards the duel that he scarcely noticed what he was eating.

Time passed. The women left to go back to the Marinetti mansion. The Leone household prepared for bed. Alone in his small room, Ned was wakeful. He had to wait until everyone was asleep, then creep out of the house. Everything would be locked, but his room was on the ground floor, and so it would be quite easy to climb out of the window. He would have to take care to dodge the Watch, or whoever it was kept order on the streets of Venice by night. He could be mistaken for a thief, or some other sort of malefactor. Or perhaps an English spy. And he'd heard Venetian prisons were hell-holes and Venetian interrogators hard and cruel. *Agh,* he thought for the hundredth time that night, *what sort of a thrice-cursed fool am I, to have let my reckless tongue run away with me and embroil me in this stupid, stupid thing!*

Also for the hundredth time that night, he took his sword out of its scabbard and looked at it. It was a good, serviceable thing, but there was nothing fancy about it. Henri d'Arcy would likely have the latest in deadly weapons. And he had probably been taught fencing, properly, from a real master, not just a demobbed soldier; he probably knew all kinds of dangerous fancy moves.

At last, Ned thought he could not delay any longer. The moon was nearly full that night, and now that the rain had stopped, the night was very clear. He slipped out through the window, left the shutters slightly ajar behind him, and set off through the nighttime streets, back to Cannaregio.

He made good time and proceeded without incident, though once or twice he had to dodge into dark doorways and behind walls to avoid a Watch patrol.

Otherwise, apart from the odd cat slinking around, the streets were deserted.

The Bosco Alley was a narrow, dingy little cobbled passage that ran between two streets. A few tall, shuttered houses lined it, cutting off nearly all the light. It was quite deserted, the cobblestones still slick from the rain. Clearly, Henri had not yet arrived. Yet somehow Ned felt very exposed there, nervous. He didn't want to wait in the open.

Just down from the corner was a deep doorway. He settled into the shadows to wait. And wait. After a while, he realized he had been so nervous that he must have arrived far too early. As the minutes crept by, the nervous tension he'd been under slowly started to relax. Tiredness crept over him. He had woken early that morning, and it was very late. His eyelids began to droop, though he tried hard to keep his eyes open. He must be ready for Henri.

Suddenly, he was jerked out of drowsiness by the creak of a door further down the alley. Then hurrying footsteps from the opposite direction. Ned's heart thudded. This was it! He was just about to step out and show himself to Henri when the hurrying footsteps ceased suddenly and a voice said softly but clearly, *'Capitano?'*

Ned was startled. That wasn't Henri's voice. It was Matthew Ashby's! What on earth was he doing here? *Has he followed me?* thought Ned. *But no, it's been at least three-quarters of an hour since I got here. What's going on?*

He peered briefly from his hiding place, taking care to keep in the shadow of the doorway. The moon had risen, and in its silver light he could see the two figures standing there, at either end of the alley. One was the unmistakeable, stout figure of Master Ashby. The other was tall, broad-shouldered, military-looking. But under his hat, he wore a half-face mask, so that Ned could see nothing of his features in the moonlight, except for a livid scar that bisected the lower part of his left cheek.

Ned's mind whirled. Ashby had said *'Capitano.'* That meant 'Captain' in Italian. Suddenly, he remembered his employer saying how his move would be to question the Ghetto guards. They were based not far away, near the canal. Yes. It made sense. This man had a military bearing. The scar on his cheek looked like an old sword-cut. He must be a captain of the guard, and Ashby must have arranged to meet him, in secret. That also explained the mask. The man didn't want passersby to see who he was.

Well! The merchant was certainly keeping his cards close to his chest, thought Ned, rather disgruntled as he remembered the way his employer had made *him* promise not to go off on private investigations.

Master Ashby came further down the alley, towards the waiting captain. As he passed Ned's hiding place, Ned kept very still. He didn't want Ashby to see him.

He could surely imagine that Ned had followed him and get really angry.

As he reached the soldier, Ashby said something cheerfully in Italian. The other man said something rapid, in a harsh voice, and Ned heard Ashby say in astonishment, '*Scusi?*'

All at once, the night seemed to erupt, as three, four, five black shapes poured from an opened window, right onto Master Ashby, who gave a little cry and went down with a thump. Without stopping to think, Ned sprang out of his hiding place, brandishing his sword. He threw himself on the back of one of the dark shapes, trying to bring him down. In the next instant he felt a ringing blow to the side of the head. In the flash of time before he crashed senseless to the ground, he saw Master Ashby struggling feebly as the dark figures tied his limbs, threw a cloth over him, and stooped rapidly to pick him up. Faintly, from far away, he heard a shout and running footsteps, then nothing.

The next thing he knew, sometime later, was the sight of a face bent over him. It was a familiar one. 'Henri!' he croaked. He tried to get up.

'Don't,' said Henri. He was flushed, as if he'd been running. 'You look terrible,' he observed. 'You've got a bruise the size of a pigeon's egg on your head.'

'Those men . . . Did you . . .'

'They ran off before I could get close to them,' said Henri briefly. 'They disappeared into that house over there. I did not fancy tackling them in there; there were rather too many of them. Besides, I didn't know how many others might be with them.' He looked at Ned. 'What happened? Why did they attack you? They didn't look like ordinary footpads.'

'Not—not me,' stammered Ned, struggling to sit up. His head swam and he saw stars. He groaned.

'I told you, lie still for a moment,' said Henri. 'You cannot do anything right now, anyway. Now tell me, what happened? Why do you say "not me"? You were the only other person I saw here.'

'The men—weren't they carrying . . .' Ned's mouth felt dry.

'I could not see clearly, but they did have a bundle wrapped in cloth, or something of the kind.' Henri's eyes narrowed. 'Do you mean to say, Ned, that you chanced upon some dark deed? Robbery? A murder?'

'Dear God, I hope not!' cried Ned, thinking of Salerio, the agent who'd been murdered by footpads. 'But he was alive when they took him, I'm sure of that. Oh, Henri, it was Master Ashby—he'd come here to meet someone, but it was a trap. I tried to help. . . .'

'And got knocked out for your pains,' said Henri. He looked thoughtful. 'They did not kill you, though they could easily have done,' he remarked. 'That's interesting.'

'Interesting,' groaned Ned, holding his sore head. 'Very interesting indeed.'

'I just mean they obviously were not intent on murder,' said Henri coolly. 'Not yours, so probably not the good Ashby's either, or they'd not have left a breathing witness. So. It follows they were most likely not hired killers, but sent on a specific mission: to capture your employer. Now, who would want to do that? And why?'

'Oh, Lord,' said Ned faintly. 'I suppose it's because he was getting too close.'

'To what?' Henri folded his arms.

Ned hesitated.

'It's no use hedging with me, Ned. You're going to have to tell me what's going on.'

'But . . .' Ned sat up very cautiously, with Henri helping him to lean against the wall. 'You and I, we were supposed to . . .'

'We can hardly fight a duel with you in that condition,' said Henri drily. 'For me, it would be too easy. Hardly honourable.'

Ned snapped, 'I can still— Ouch!' He broke off, wincing. 'My head really hurts.'

'We can always fight the duel some other time, if you really insist,' said Henri lightly. 'But for now we must try and help your employer. Do you agree?'

'Yes,' whispered Ned.

'We must trust each other in this, at least,' said Henri. 'Do you agree?'

Ned searched the young Frenchman's face. Slowly, reluctantly, he nodded.

'Very well. Then you must tell me what happened,' said Henri.

Ned said, 'You must swear to keep it a secret. You must swear, on the thing most sacred to you.'

Henri's dark eyes regarded him assessingly. 'I swear on the Virgin Mary and the memory of my mother,' he said softly. He held out a hand to Ned.

As they shook hands, the eyes of the two young men met and Ned knew, without a doubt, that he had grossly misjudged Henri d'Arcy in the past. The young Frenchman could have been a friend, if Ned himself had not been so aggressive and suspicious. He said quietly, 'Thank you.'

'What for?' said Henri, raising an eyebrow.

'For tonight. Coming to my aid.'

'I didn't think of it that way.' Henri shrugged. 'I was late for our meeting—my father's dinner guests didn't leave for hours, and I couldn't slip out of the house, and I was hurrying. Then when I turned the corner into the alley and saw those black crows and you lying on the ground, why, I didn't stop to think, I just ran! I'm just sorry I didn't catch up to them before they got away.'

'If only I'd been in a fit state,' said Ned, 'I could have helped you chase them and we might—'

'With mights and ifs, we could put all Paris in a bottle,'

observed Henri. 'No. There were too many of them, even for both of us.'

'We could have gone for help.'

'From whom? Didn't you notice—with all that commotion, not one window in this alley opened, not one door. The inhabitants must be used to keeping their ears and eyes shut. There would be no help from them.' He smiled suddenly and the smile lightened up his whole face. 'So, Ned Fletcher, we bury our quarrel, just for now, yes?'

'Yes,' said Ned. He added wonderingly, 'It is a strange thing, though—if you and I had not decided to fight a duel this night, at this place, then I should never have seen what happened to Master Ashby. I would be asleep in my bed, not knowing anything till the morning.'

'And there would have been no trail to follow, nothing,' said Henri, smiling. 'It is true, Ned. Fate works in strange ways, does it not?'

'Yes,' agreed Ned soberly, and then he began to tell Henri about what had happened, from events in London to that night. Henri listened without interruption or comment. When Ned had finished, the other said quietly, 'There are two choices as to who kidnapped your master: the pirates or their paymasters, or the Montemoros.'

'Yes,' said Ned. 'But of the two, I think the Montemoros are more likely. You see, I think the pirates would just have killed him, just like they killed Salerio. But the Montemoros would just want to know what he knows.

Whether he knows where Sarah is, for instance. And so they'd want to question him, not kill him.'

Henri nodded. 'Yes. That seems fair enough. You think Master Ashby came here to speak to the guards in secret?'

'Yes.'

'I do not think those black crows were guards,' said Henri.

'No,' said Ned. 'I think they must have been sent by the Countess. She must have heard about Master Ashby's visit to the Ghetto. Maybe someone saw him and reported it to the Countess.'

'Possibly,' said Henri.

Ned got to his feet. His head was still throbbing, though not as badly as before. 'We've got to rescue him.'

Henri shook his head decisively. 'What, go to that house? We'd be captured too, if not killed.'

'But he's Celia's father! And he's at the mercy of those creatures. . . .'

'I doubt they'll harm him,' said Henri firmly. 'The Countess will want him in good health to answer questions. Besides, she must know who he is, or else how would he have been lured here? Then she'll know he's a subject of your Queen and that he has influential contacts here as well. It would not be wise of her to kill or injure him. She's not like those pirates who killed Salerio. She is from a prominent family with a good deal to lose if she gets involved in the murder of a well-connected foreigner.'

'Anyway,' said Ned impatiently, 'if we can't go to that house, we must go and tell Dr Leone at once. He's clever, and I know he's got powerful friends. He said so. He'll know what to do.' He had never felt like this before, he thought, amazed at himself: strong, clear, decisive, and in control. It was a pleasant feeling, despite his anxiety about Master Ashby.

Questions

Dr Leone's house was still dark and quiet when the two young men climbed back in through Ned's bedroom window. They raced up the stairs to Dr Leone's second-floor bedroom and tapped lightly on the door. There was no answer. They tapped louder. Still no answer.

'He must be asleep,' said Henri.

'We'll have to wake him anyway,' said Ned. They tried the door. It was unlocked. They went in.

Dr Leone was not in his room. The bed was rumpled,

but he was not in it. The two young men looked at each other. Where could he be? Then Ned had an idea.

'Today, when he was telling us about his work, he mentioned that he sometimes got ideas in the middle of the night and then he just went up to his laboratory to work when everyone was asleep. He said he'd had all those rooms upstairs constructed with double layers of wood and rags, so that the sounds would be deadened and no one would be woken up. I wager that's where he is.'

'Let's go and check, then,' said Henri.

Sure enough, there was a thin bar of yellow light under the laboratory door. Ned tried the door. It was locked, but by putting his ear to it he could hear someone moving about. He knocked.

There was a moment's silence from inside the room; then Dr Leone's voice came sharply. 'Who's that?'

'Me, sir. Ned Fletcher.'

'Ned! Wait a moment.' There came a bang, a scrape, then footsteps approaching the door. It opened. Dr Leone's face peered crossly out.

'What in God's name are you doing up at this time of night?' Then the alchemist caught sight of Henri. 'And who is this? What is going on?'

'Henri d'Arcy, at your service,' said Henri, bowing.

'What? Wasn't it a d'Arcy who brought Mateo and the rest of you here?'

'Yes, sir, Henri has—'

'What are you two doing, gallivanting around at

night?' demanded Dr Leone. 'And what do you mean by disturbing me? I was just about to test an idea and now you've interrupted me.'

'Forgive us, Dr Leone,' said Ned, 'but this is really important. Master Ashby—he's been taken prisoner.'

'What?' Dr Leone opened the door and came out of the laboratory, shutting the door behind him. 'Are you drunk or dreaming, Ned? Mateo is asleep in his bed.'

'Forgive me, sir, but that isn't so. He's been taken prisoner by masked men. We think they are in the service of the Countess of Montemoro.'

Dr Leone looked quite bewildered. 'What nonsense is this?' He looked from one face to the other, and for the first time seemed to notice Ned's state. 'Why, lad, you look terrible, as if someone has taken to you with a cudgel!'

'And that's not so far from the truth,' said Ned grimly. 'Dr Leone, you must listen to us. We must help Master Ashby.'

And he told the alchemist what had happened, except for why he'd been there. At the end, Dr Leone said slowly, 'This is a fantastic story. It beggars belief!'

'I assure you, sir, it's all true,' said Ned.

'But he said nothing to me about going to meet this supposed captain of guards! I never heard of any message telling him to meet this character at the Bosco Alley!'

'Perhaps he was told not to tell anyone,' said Henri.

'But I'm his friend and I've been helping him. We interviewed Dr Tedeschi together. So why didn't the message come for both of us, luring us out there? Why take only Mateo?'

'I don't know,' said Ned, 'but perhaps they thought you would not be fooled by it.' He glanced at Dr Leone's imposing bulk. 'Or perhaps they thought you'd be too difficult to capture quietly.'

'Or that you didn't know as much as Master Ashby,' suggested Henri.

'All three are possible,' agreed Dr Leone. 'But there is yet another possibility. It may have nothing to do with the Tedeschi case at all, but with the pirates.'

'I don't think so, sir,' said Ned crisply, and explained his reasons.

Dr Leone nodded. 'You may well be right. But lads, before we take this any further, you understand that I must check to see that this isn't just some strange dream you've been having.' And he locked the door of the laboratory behind him and set off at a run down the stairs, taking them two at a time—followed by Ned and Henri.

The door to Master Ashby's room, on the first floor, was shut but not locked. They went in. Dr Leone stood stock-still in the middle of the room, looking at the empty bed, the open window, the twisted sheet tied to the catch of the shutters. 'Mother of God,' he whispered, 'he must have climbed down the sheet. In his state of fitness! He could have broken a leg!'

Ned felt absurdly proud of his employer. 'He is a much nimbler man than you might suppose, sir,' he said, 'and braver.'

'Of that last quality I have no doubt,' said Dr Leone. He sat down heavily on the bed. 'Well, it seems you were right. At least, it seems he's gone off into the night. Quite who took him—that's a different matter.' His eyes narrowed. 'But you haven't explained one thing, young Ned.' He shot a glance at Henri. 'Or you, Monsieur d'Arcy, come to that. What were you doing at the Bosco Alley at that time of night?'

'I . . . we . . . that is, Henri and I, we had arranged to meet.' Ned's face flamed. 'We were going to fight a duel.'

'A what?' said Dr Leone faintly, looking at Ned as though he were mad.

'A duel,' said Henri calmly. 'Ned and I—well, we'd had a disagreement. We were going to sort it out that way. That's all.'

'And now?'

'Now, we've agreed to shelve our quarrel. There are more important things at the moment, Dr Leone.'

'I see. Very wise. A duel! What foolishness. You would do well to forget such things completely. Well now, let's see . . . We need reinforcements. We will go and pay a visit to a captain of the Watch, who's the son of a friend of mine. He might be able to bring some of his men with us, to go to that house on Bosco Alley.'

'But, sir, if you tell him why—'

'Not a word about the Tedeschis—or indeed pirates—shall pass my lips. I'll just tell him I have had a good friend abducted by malefactors and held in that house. It's not altogether uncommon for such things to happen. Occasionally foreign merchants and the like are kidnapped and held to ransom by armed gangs. Usually they're from the outer islands, but even in the city, it's been known to happen. We'll go there and demand entry.'

'What if they refuse?' said Ned.

'Then we storm the house,' said Dr Leone calmly. 'But I don't think it'll come to that. Not if entry is demanded in the name of the Duke.'

'What if they've moved Master Ashby from the house?' said Henri.

'Well, then we'll have to think of something else,' said Dr Leone. 'Just give me a minute and I'll be ready. We'll set off at once. The Watch-house is only two or three streets away.'

The Captain of the Watch was a hard-faced young man only a few years older than Henri and Ned. He sat at a table with several of his men, playing cards. He listened to what Ned thought must be Dr Leone's carefully edited story without a flicker of expression, then said something rapidly in Italian. Dr Leone answered, fluttering his hands about, gesturing to Ned and Henri. The

Captain looked steadily at them without speaking; then he said something sharp and rough. Henri flushed. He saw Ned's bemusement and said, 'He says we're fools. Duelling is forbidden in such circumstances. We should have had seconds, and it should have been out in the open, and in the day.'

'Oh,' said Ned, 'but if we'd done that, everyone would have known.'

'Don't worry about it,' said Henri, shrugging. The Captain had turned back to Dr Leone and seemed to be consulting with him. Henri whispered, 'They're negotiating. It's highly irregular, he says, but he'll do it, for a financial consideration.'

'Of course,' said Ned wryly. 'Who ever heard of men-at-arms doing things for love?'

In the end, and after much haggling, the Captain came with four of his men, all burly young fellows who looked like they might certainly be handy in a fight. And so it was that they went back to Cannaregio to the relentless rhythm of the tramp, tramp, tramp of the men of the Watch.

WOLF'S DEN

The house stood dark and quiet. The alley, and the streets near it, were perfectly still and empty. The inhabitants were either asleep or lying low.

Bang, bang, bang! The Captain was no respecter of people's sleep. 'Open up, in the name of the Duke!' he roared in Italian. Ned didn't need anyone to translate. It was perfectly plain.

There was silence. 'Open in the name of the Duke!' roared the Captain again.

A shutter creaked open. A tousled dark head peered out of a first-floor window. A voice croaked a question.

The Captain shouted back, 'In the name of the Duke!'

The head nodded and disappeared. In a few moments they heard someone fumbling with the bolts on the heavy door. The door creaked open to reveal a young man of about twenty, with sleepy eyes and a determined chin. He stared at them and said something in Italian. The Captain snapped something back.

'He's saying he has reason to suspect a crime's been committed and that the criminals are hiding here,' whispered Henri to Ned.

The young man launched into voluble denials, which the Captain cut off with an eloquent gesture, indicating to the young man he should stand aside and let them in.

He shrugged and did as he was told, sulkily.

Once inside, the Captain sent his men to search the rooms. Dr Leone went with him. But he asked Henri and Ned to stay with the young man, in case he should try to escape, or raise the alarm. The latter sat on the floor with his back to the wall, looking anywhere but at the other two young men. Ned and Henri conferred in low voices.

'Do you recognize him? Is he one of the men who attacked Master Ashby?' asked Henri.

'Can't tell. They wore masks. It's not the one with the scar, I'll wager. But it could be one of the others. I hardly saw them.'

Henri turned to their prisoner. 'Who are you?'

The other looked at him for a moment, dark eyes unfathomable; then he shrugged and looked away.

'He won't tell us anything,' said Ned. 'But it does not matter. The others . . .'

At that moment, Dr Leone came back. 'There seems to be no one here, except an old man who was in bed and that youth,' he said in English. 'He claims to be the youth's father and says they live here alone. The Captain's men are searching the attics. Are you sure it was this house?'

'Quite sure,' said Henri and Ned together.

'Well, let's hope, then, that—' began Dr Leone as the Captain and his men clattered into the hall, followed by a rather frail-looking old man in nightcap and nightshirt. The youth immediately leaped towards him. 'Papa!'

Ned was going to stop him but was halted by an imperious gesture from the Captain, who then turned to Dr Leone and barked out some words.

'He says there's no one in the attics either,' said Henri. 'He's not very happy. He thinks he was sent on a wild-goose chase.'

'It was no wild-goose chase,' said Ned indignantly. 'You saw them go in here!'

'Maybe then he's already been taken away,' said Dr Leone, brightening. 'The backwater near here is an offshoot of the big canal, so it'd be quite easy to be far away in a matter of minutes.' He turned to the Captain, who rapped something back. Dr Leone snorted in disbelief.

'The Captain says the old man told him they have no boat,' explained Henri. 'Dr Leone said that was a lie, no household in Venice was without a boat.'

Dr Leone spoke again. The Captain shrugged. Henri said, 'He's saying there's no one here, that we must have been mistaken.'

Dr Leone tried to speak again, but the Captain brushed him off. Dr Leone sighed, and turned to Ned and Henri. 'I'm sorry, lads. We have to leave.'

'But . . . but we haven't asked these people here any questions!' said Ned. 'They're hiding something, I'm sure they are!'

'The Captain says he talked at length to the old man. He says they're just ordinary people. He says it's clear that not only is there no one else here now, but there was no one else here tonight at all. He says that you two are just confused, or troublemakers. I tell you, he's pretty annoyed,' said Dr Leone ruefully.

'But—'

'I'm sorry, Ned,' said Dr Leone. 'But there's nothing we can do.'

Ned blurted out, 'No! We can't just let—'

The Captain put a heavy hand on his shoulder. *'Andiamo,'* he said. Let's go. And his tone left no doubt that he would brook no opposition whatsoever. So, reluctantly, Ned and Henri allowed themselves to be propelled out of the doorway and back out into the street, while the youth and his father clung together, the very picture of wrongly accused innocence.

There was nothing more they could do in Bosco Alley tonight. Even if Matthew Ashby was still there in the house—which was unlikely, as the search had been pretty thorough—the villains had been alerted and would move him as soon as possible. No, said Dr Leone, they would have to change tactics, and go for a really bold move.

'I think we must beard the she-wolf in her den,' he said. 'Tomorrow morning we will go and call on the Montemoros.'

'What, and just ask the Countess to give us back Master Ashby?' cried Ned.

'I'm not quite as bold as that,' said Dr Leone, laughing. 'No, we will go to the Count as petitioners, and ask humbly for his help in locating our imprudent friend, who was kidnapped by a gang of island pirates while trying to investigate their crimes.'

'Won't it look strange, going to the Count for help in a matter like this?'

'Not at all. He fancies himself as a protector of the city. And pirates are a plague—everyone knows that. Especially wealthy and powerful families. Venice is wealthy from its trade. Pirates threaten that wealth. The Montemoros have never had to suffer directly from them, but I'm sure they hate such people as much as anybody does.

It makes the perfect cover for our enquiries into the Tedeschi case.' He paused. 'Besides, it may in fact be the case that Mateo has really been kidnapped by the pirates he was investigating.'

'But, sir, remember what we discussed! The pirates would surely have killed my master. Think how cruel they are—they haven't let one crew-member from the seized ships escape death. And they murdered Salerio, just in case he was getting too close. No, he'd be dead if it were them. Besides, you and Master Ashby had just gone to see Dr Tedeschi. And he spoke of wanting to interview the guards about Sarah. So it must be that!'

Dr Leone shrugged. 'Possibly. Though I'm not sure. Anyway, the pirate angle is what we must present to the Count.'

'But what if the Countess hears of our attempt to enlist her husband's help?'

'What of it? It'll flush her out into the open. And we can see how she reacts. What's more, if we can persuade the Count to go looking for Master Ashby's kidnappers, the Countess will think twice about continuing to hold him—if indeed it is she who holds him.' He turned to Henri. 'You might do best staying at my house tonight, young man. We will send a message to your father first thing to tell him where you are. Will that be suitable?'

'Absolutely,' said Henri, eyes shining. 'I wouldn't miss going to the Montemoros' for the world.'

'And no duelling in my house,' said Dr Leone sharply.

'Oh, that will be for quite another place and time, if it happens,' said Henri coolly. 'Don't you agree, Ned?'

'Mmm,' said Ned absently. His mind was on other things. 'Dr Leone, we've got to tell Celia and Mistress Quickly what's happened.'

Dr Leone shook his head. 'No. Not until we've been to see the Montemoros.'

'Then Celia will want to come with us. She hates being kept out of things. And she's clever,' said Ned.

The other two looked at him in some surprise. Dr Leone laughed gustily. 'My dear Ned, women have to be shown a firm hand, you know. Especially one as reckless as Miss Celia. Don't tell her where we're going. Make up a story of some sort.'

Blushing but determined, Ned said, 'I can't tell her anything of the kind. I don't want to lie to her. It's not fair.'

Dr Leone raised his eyebrows. 'Such scruples! Very well. We won't lie to her. We'll leave very early, long before anyone else is up. Then nobody need lie, except the servants. Now then, I think a little sleep is called for, or our brains will turn to porridge.'

Ned thought he would never be able to go to sleep. So he was surprised when he suddenly started awake out of a dreamless, heavy slumber, Henri shaking him and whispering, 'Get up. Hurry. It's time we were going. Dr Leone's got the boat ready.'

It was a grey morning again, the mist lying on the

canal, but not rainy. Already there was a good deal of traffic on the waterways, for Venice was a city of business, and business woke early. It was a busy, colourful scene, with boats laden with goods from trading ships anchored at the Rialto wharves; market boats, filled with vegetables and fruit; passenger boats, ferrying people from one part of the city to another; private boats belonging to great families . . .

Like many of Venice's noble families, the Montemoros had their palace directly fronting the Grand Canal. It was a beautiful three-storey building of marble and stucco, built two centuries before and decorated with rounded windows, delicate balconies, and fresh new frescoes. There was a large arched watergate down below, the arch prominently emblazoned with the rather sinister emblem of the Montemoros—a black wolf's head, against a sharp peaked hill. Here, boats could come directly in to moor under shelter. The palace spoke not only of great wealth, but of confident power. It was all very well to talk bravely about going up against such power, Ned thought; it was quite another to actually come up against it. With a sudden shudder, he thought: *Here we are, gliding right into the wolf's den.*

But the wolf was obviously drowsy that morning, for the gondola got very close indeed to the palace before anyone seemed to notice. Then a small boat, with two guards in it, came out of the watergate towards them.

They called out a challenge and Dr Leone answered calmly.

'He's saying we're here to present a petition to the Count, that we have been the victims of kidnap gangs and that we crave his most gracious help,' translated Henri to Ned.

The guards' boat drew up alongside. Their suspicious glances swept over the alchemist, then the two young men. *'Il nome,'* one of them barked. Your name.

Dr Leone told them. He added something, in fluent tones. 'He's saying the Count knows him well, that he's the most famous alchemist in Venice and that if they know what's good for them, they'll go straight away and tell him we're here,' said Henri.

The guards must have been impressed, for they turned around and went swiftly back to the palace.

Within a very short time they were back and spoke to Dr Leone, who nodded, smiling.

'It's worked,' he said to Ned and Henri. 'He'll give us a few minutes of his time. We're in, lads.'

As the gondola sailed in under the arches of the Montemoro palace, Ned's heart gave a little skip of mingled excitement and nervousness. Yes, they were in the wolf's den now. But they'd better take care. Very great care. For even if the wolf was drowsy, everyone knew that in fact it was the she-wolf who could be the most dangerous enemy.

Part Two

A DARK WEB

Celia woke that morning with a headache. She'd had an agitated night, with lots of unpleasant dreams, and didn't feel rested at all. She lay there for a little while, rubbing at her temples, trying to relax enough to go back to sleep, but she couldn't. A sense of nameless dread filled her. She hated the feeling. She was a practical girl, not an imaginative one. Leave a wisp of dream to Ned and he'd spin a story for you out of nothing. But she prided herself on her common sense. Her calm. Her understanding of real life. And yet underlying the nightmares that had plagued her was the sense that something was wrong. Something didn't make sense. They'd missed something. And now as she lay there, uneasily, she suddenly knew what it was. It was a question they should have asked themselves from the beginning.

Why, if his daughter had been accused of witchcraft and then disappeared, had Dr Tedeschi been left free and unmolested? Why hadn't the Countess had him arrested? Of course, she might not have known Sarah had disappeared straight away. But it was at least seven weeks since her disappearance, and surely in that time the Countess would have found out if she had an informer in the Ghetto, as Dr Leone suspected. A girl can't just vanish without it attracting attention from her neighbours. And by all accounts Sarah had not been a stay-at-home, but helped her father on his visits to patients. Her absence would have been noticed. Then the first thing the Countess might have done was to haul in Sarah's father for questioning. She would have suspected he knew where his daughter was. But he had not been touched; and that, thought Celia, was surely strange. The woman was apparently obsessed with witchcraft and sorcery—not only had she accused Sarah, but she'd also accused Dr Leone, earlier. She was apparently a fanatic; so why wouldn't she try all means to run the witch to ground, including leaning on her father?

It could only mean one thing, thought Celia, sitting bolt upright in bed. It must mean that the witchcraft accusation was a blind and that the Countess was after Sarah *for quite some other reason*. There was the obvious solution, of course: the Count had fallen in love with the girl, his wife had seen it, and, insanely jealous, she sought to destroy her. But why in this way? Why not just have the girl murdered by some hired killer, before she even suspected the Countess's hatred? That would be easy enough for a person in the Countess's position to arrange. It was true the Jews of Venice were protected by law from molestation, but you could make such a thing look like an ordinary street crime. It wasn't uncommon for footpads to kill people in the course of a robbery, and the murders were very often not solved, especially if the person concerned had been of no social consequence.

Instead, the Countess had accused Sarah of being a witch. *But not to the authorities*. If it had been a formal accusation to the Council of Ten, then Venetian justice would have swung into action. The girl would have been arrested, tried, sentenced if found guilty, acquitted if found innocent. Perhaps.

But nothing like this had happened. Sarah had disappeared, but there had been no official hue and cry. Only the Countess, looking for her . . . Therefore it meant there had still been no formal, public accusation. It must have come as a private communication, then, verbal or written. Which meant the Countess must not be quite sure of her ground with the Council of Ten, or of making her accusation stick in the full glare of a public trial.

Which then meant first of all, thought Celia, that the Tedeschis were not bereft of influence and not so easily accused. But also that the Countess was gambling on the idea that such an accusation would frighten the young and inexperienced Sarah into precipitous action. Yes, perhaps that was the whole idea—*to frighten Sarah into vanishing*. Because then she might either vanish for good—might be so scared she would leave the city and never come back—or the Countess would have the leisure to look for her and, if she found her, question her in private and then dispose of her, permanently and quietly. Which meant, thought Celia excitedly as she hurriedly dressed and ran a comb through her hair, that the Countess felt threatened by Sarah, but that she wasn't sure how much. She suspected Sarah might know something. Something important. Something that directly incriminated the Countess, in some way.

But what? Whatever it was, it could not have been something Dr Tedeschi could know, or he would have been picked up by the Countess's men. Celia thought hard. The accusation had come the day after the Tedeschis had been at the Montemoros', seeing to that patient. What if Sarah alone had seen something which incriminated the Countess and the woman had realized that? Dr Tedeschi had said that Sarah had been left alone for a short while at his patient's bedside while he went to mix medicines. This was when she had briefly met the Count. *But what if it was nothing to do with the Count at all?* What if it was something Sarah had seen while she sat at the patient's bedside?

The patient had been an elderly woman, some sort of cousin of the Countess's. On the face of it, thought Celia, not a significant person. What if it was not to do with the patient, though, but the room in which she lay? Could Sarah have seen something out of a window, for instance? Or overheard something she wasn't meant to?

Yes, thought Celia. That *must* be why the girl had disappeared—because after she was accused she had realized the significance of what she'd witnessed. She had said she was the 'victim of a conspiracy.'

That must be what it was about! *My God, what a dark web we have stumbled into.*

I must tell Father at once, she thought as she went out of the room, headache quite forgotten. *We must go and see Dr Tedeschi and ask him questions about that room and what Sarah might possibly have witnessed while she was in it.*

Mistress Quickly was already up, having breakfast, when Celia went downstairs. 'You look rather tired,' Mistress Quickly observed as Celia sat down at the table. 'You'd best have a restful day, after all that silly nonsense yesterday.'

'Aunt Bess,' said Celia, ignoring this comment, 'did

Father say anything to you about whether Dr Tedeschi told him exactly what happened when Sarah was left alone at the patient's bedside?'

Mistress Quickly stared at her. 'Goodness me, child, it's rather early in the morning for this.'

'But did he?'

'No, but then why should he?' She snorted and reached for another piece of bread, which she buttered thickly. 'This whole business is absurd, it seems to me. Matthew has enough on his plate without worrying about this sordid affair. It's much more important that he deal with this piracy business, which is dangerous enough without adding to it. Besides, it's quite clear to me what happened with that girl. The Countess Montemoro took a set against her because of her husband's roving eye. And the girl's had the good sense to make herself scarce. If she has even more sense, she's far away from here by now and we're on a wild-goose chase. Which is Matthew all over, of course. Can't resist a story of injustice, even more when it's recounted by a pretty woman like Emilia Lanier.'

Celia smiled at her aunt's vehemence. 'But, Aunt Bess, you know Sarah sent her father a note just recently. She's still around, she's still in danger from that Montemoro woman, and Father still wants to help her.'

'Exactly. That brother of mine could think a bit more of those closer to him than a pack of strangers,' said Mistress Quickly tartly. 'Why multiply your enemies?

Piracy's a big-enough tangle to be involved in. He is much too fond of rushing into things.' She gave Celia a sideways glance. 'He's not the only one. Your Ned does not look very far before he leaps either.'

Celia stared at her. 'He's not *my* Ned.'

'Fiddlesticks,' said Bess Quickly. 'Yours for the asking. Your worshipful servant.'

Celia went red as suddenly something else fell into place. Something she should have known all along. Something that, quite unexpectedly, made her heart skip a beat. She faltered. 'No. No. You're quite wrong. He just sees me as a little girl, as his adopted sister or something. Besides, he thinks I'm frivolous, empty-headed—'

'Rubbish. He's head over heels in love with you, silly girl,' said her aunt. 'I've seen it coming for months.'

'Oh.' Celia's pulse beat fast. 'I . . . I didn't know . . . I . . .'

'Listen to me, Celia. Ned thinks he's not good enough and that your father wants a wealthy man for you. I don't think that's true; but he has been too modest to speak his mind to you, or to your father. Don't treat him badly, whatever you feel about him.'

'Why should I treat him badly?' cried Celia, nettled. 'He is my best friend. The best friend I could ever have.'

'That's a start,' said Bess. 'But he wants more than your friendship, my girl. What do you feel about that?'

Celia was silent an instant. This new vision of Ned as

a possible lover was a kind of shock, but not an unpleasant one. No. There was a strange warmth in her body, a kind of sweetness in her limbs, that she'd never experienced before. She said quietly, 'I . . . I don't know.'

'Fair enough,' said her aunt placidly. 'Don't rush into things, that's my advice. Know your own mind. But Ned knows his, and that I'd wager on, and win. He's a determined young man, that one, for all his dreams. Now, never mind that for the moment. What are your plans for today?'

Still a little shaky, Celia said, 'I—I thought I'd go over and see the others, ask Father about Dr Tedeschi, and—'

Mistress Quickly made an impatient gesture. 'Pish, not more of that stuff. We're in Venice. I want to see it. I thought we could go for a ride down the Grand Canal. The Marinettis have a very comfortable gondola, and the housekeeper said it has been put at our disposal, as has the boatman. She said she can prepare a fine picnic lunch for us and we can go and explore the city from the comfort of a boat.'

'I thought you didn't like boats, Aunt Bess,' said Celia, smiling, remembering her aunt's seasickness on the ship that had brought them here.

'I don't like the sea,' said Mistress Quickly. 'I don't think I'd even like the lagoon much. But the Grand Canal is a different matter. What do you say?'

'I thought that I should . . . ,' began Celia, but she saw

her aunt's hurt expression and changed tack immediately. 'Yes, why not? It would be a nice thing to do.' She hesitated, blushed, and raced on. 'Could I perhaps—I mean, could Ned come with us?'

Her aunt smiled and patted her arm. 'Of course, my dear. If that's what you want. But tell him not to be late. There's a good deal to see, they tell me.'

'I'll go over now to tell him. And I'll tell him to make sure he's not late, Aunt Bess,' said Celia, planting a kiss on her aunt's cheek. There was a bubble of excitement inside her, a sudden thrill of delightful power.

A quizzical smile on her lips, Bess Quickly watched her go. Had she done the right thing, pointing out the obvious to her niece? She hoped so. She liked Ned. She hoped Celia wouldn't be a minx and play games with his heart, now the truth was revealed to her. It had certainly taken her long enough to see it. Of course, the child had no imagination to speak of. Feet on the ground, Celia had, and that was good. But a touch of magic was what she needed, so those feet wouldn't be too earthbound, the heart too solidly full of common sense. And magic that strange lad had, Bess thought, that was certain. A magic she'd wager he didn't even know he had . . .

'Sorry, signorina,' said Dr Leone's servant, 'but the young gentleman left early this morning. He and the other young gentleman, and Dr Leone, they—'

'Which other young gentleman?' said Celia sharply.

'A friend of Signore Fletcher's, I believe. Or perhaps Dr Leone's? I am not sure, signorina.'

'My father—' began Celia.

'He too has gone, signorina.'

Celia stared at him. 'You mean, they're *all* out, at *this* hour?'

'Yes, signorina.'

'Where did they go?'

'I do not know, signorina. But they took the boat. No boatman, though—Dr Leone was going to row himself.'

'But what direction did they go in?'

'I did not see, signorina. I am sorry.'

Celia stared crossly at the man's impassive face, the bubble of delight quite burst inside her now. 'I'll wager you know more than you're saying,' she snapped. 'They told you to keep it quiet, didn't they?'

The man said nothing.

'Of all the dirty tricks,' said Celia furiously. 'They've gone off investigating something, I'll wager my little finger. And they thought it would be too dangerous for me, I suppose! Men!'

'Scusi?' said the servant, sounding bewildered, and Celia realized that in her agitation she must have spoken in English. Switching quickly to Italian, she said, 'Well, can you tell them, when they return, that Mistress Quickly and I have also gone out and that we will not be returning till late.'

The man nodded. 'Where shall I say you are going, signorina?'

'You can say you don't know and that you're sorry,' said Celia coldly, turning on her heel and walking away. What cheek! What meanness! Father she could understand; he was old and inclined to be fussy. Dr Leone was an overbearing Venetian gallant, used to getting his own way and treating women as if they were glass ornaments that could be smashed.

But Ned—how could he do this to her, keep her in the dark, if what Aunt Bess said was true? He *knew* what it meant to her to be part of this investigation. If he really did love her, he'd have thought of her. He'd have told her. Perhaps he'd been persuaded by the others, she thought—but then that meant he was weak. And you didn't want weakness in a lover. You wanted courage. Strength. Thoughtfulness. And tenderness. None of these Ned had shown by going off like this, betraying her. . . . And it hurt. It hurt like hot needles in her flesh.

She brushed those thoughts angrily aside. Why should she care what Ned thought, what he felt about her? She felt only exasperation towards him right now, nothing more. Nothing! She wouldn't think about him. Now, who was the other young man? The servant did not seem to know him.

An idea struck her. What if he was the man they had been looking for yesterday? Sarah's friend, who had hidden her? It would explain their sudden departure, if he had come to them and told them who he was—and that he could take them to Sarah. Or—and here her heart pounded—what if he was the man she'd talked to yesterday, the wolfish young man in Cannaregio? Perhaps he knew something, or pretended to. *Perhaps,* she thought—*perhaps it's* they *who are in danger!*

But Dr Leone was no fool, and he knew Venice and Venetians. He'd been angry yesterday because he thought the young man might be an informer. He'd hardly follow someone like that, like a fly blundering into a spider's web. No, it could not be that young man. It must be someone with real information about Sarah, something they had to check out straight away. They'd had to take the boat—so it must be too far, or too complicated, to walk to.

Well, Celia thought, defiantly, as she marched back to the Marinetti house, *Aunt Bess and I have a boat too—and we're not only going to swan down the Grand Canal, gawking at palaces. The Cannaregio canal is nice and wide and there's lots to see along it. And if we come close to the Ghetto bridge, that will be a good place to stop and moor. I'll think of something to persuade Aunt Bess that we must go and pay our respects to the good Dr Tedeschi. And then we'll see who's ahead!*

But it still rankled, and bitterly, that they should not have involved her in what was obviously an important development. She was a member of this mission just as they were. Certainly just as much as Ned! She was no shrinking violet, no delicate flower. Why should she have to prove herself, just because she was a girl? Why should Ned be trusted to help and not her? It wasn't fair. Well, she would show them!

THE SHE-WOLF

The room into which Ned, Henri, and Dr Leone were ushered to wait for the Count was large and spacious, with a gloriously painted ceiling and bright frescoes on the walls. The only bits of furniture were four chairs against one wall.

It was an ordinary-enough room, yet there was something about it that made Ned feel uneasy. He felt as though unseen eyes were watching him. But there was no one there except themselves, and no obvious spy-holes.

Suddenly the door at the end of the room opened.

A guard came out. 'The Count will see you now,' he said, and ushered them through.

This room too had an odd atmosphere. Perhaps because it was so stuffy and heavily decorated—the walls painted in red and gold, with pictures crammed on every square inch of them. There was a good deal of carved, gilded furniture, including an ornate desk and chair. Over the desk hung a striking portrait of a man dressed in the fashion of the previous century. And at the desk, under the painting, sat a man who could almost have been the twin of the man in the portrait. He was about forty-five, tall, broad-shouldered, auburn-haired, and tawny-eyed, with a bony face and a big nose, and wearing the plain dark robes of the high Venetian aristocracy.

'Buongiorno, signore.' The Count's voice was soft and held little inflection. Ned could see the deep lines etched into his face, the dark circles under his eyes, the threads of silver that ran through the auburn hair, the way his fingers drummed nervously on the desk. *He looks jumpy, haunted, unhappy,* thought Ned suddenly. *As if there is something weighing on him.*

The Count motioned for them to sit down and for the guard to go away. The man hesitated perceptibly; then he bowed and left the room, closing the door behind him.

The Count said something to Dr Leone, who took a parchment from his doublet and handed it to the Count. The Count perused it briefly. Ned knew it was the document that Dr Leone had concocted last night, detailing the supposed kidnap of Master Ashby by 'island pirates.'

He asked a question. Dr Leone answered. The Count frowned and glanced towards Ned and Henri. Dr Leone said something rapidly, no doubt explaining their part in it. They'd decided to keep as close to the truth as possible. When the doctor had finished, the Count was silent a moment. Then he spoke quickly to Dr Leone.

'He wants to ask you questions,' said the doctor, turning to Ned, 'as you're Master Ashby's employee and were on the spot when he was taken. I'll translate and convey your answers.'

The Count spoke. Dr Leone said, with a slightly raised eyebrow, 'He asks if you've known Master Ashby long.'

'Of course,' said Ned. 'He's my master. I've worked for him for years.'

The Count's gaze rested on Ned, rather disapprovingly. He said something querulous. Dr Leone hesitated a moment, then said, 'The Count asks, is your master a spy for Queen Elizabeth?'

Ned stared. 'What?'

Dr Leone repeated the question.

Ned stammered, 'Dr Leone, you—you must tell him that's not true. Master Ashby has never been a spy! He's a well-respected merchant!'

'Don't fret, Ned. I know.'

Dr Leone turned back to the Count. More querulous words from the noble man.

'The Count says that just because Master Ashby is a merchant doesn't mean he isn't also spying,' Dr Leone reported back. 'He says there have been one or two English merchants who have been caught doing exactly that. And they paid for it in Venetian prisons.'

'Sir, you must convince him that it isn't so! We came to . . . so he could visit you, and . . . and investigate the pirates,' cried Ned. *How foolish we are to have come here,* he thought, shivering. *We are well and truly in the wolf's den now. We could end up in a Venetian prison ourselves. Or worse still, on the rack.*

'Hush,' said Dr Leone, and turning back to the Count, he spoke volubly and fluently. The Count listened. His eyes fixed on Ned, he spoke again.

'He asks if your master is working for someone else,' the doctor translated.

'What? Who could he be working for? Only the group of merchants to which he belongs, back in England.'

Dr Leone said calmly, 'I told him that. But he asks if you've been paid to snoop on him.'

Ned swallowed. 'Dr Leone, I don't understand. What sorts of questions are these?'

'Those of a man who doesn't trust people much, I'd say,' said Dr Leone lightly. To the Count, he spoke soothing words in Italian.

The Count answered quickly. Dr Leone translated. 'He says, what was the English merchant looking for, in the alley, at that time of night?'

'An informant arranged to meet him—someone who had something important to tell him, about the pirates we told him about,' said Ned, trying to sound convincing, and Dr Leone conveyed it to the Count.

Montemoro shot a hard glance at Ned. Then he said something, to which Dr Leone responded, spreading his hands and shrugging his shoulders.

Henri whispered, 'The Count wanted to know why Master Ashby didn't take anyone along for protection on such a dangerous undertaking. Informants are often criminals themselves and not to be trusted. Dr Leone said he was a trusting man. Too trusting.'

'That's right,' said Ned, brightening. 'He's a good man. A kind man. Tell him that, Dr Leone. It's not a crime, to be trusting.'

Dr Leone turned back to the Count, who nodded and smiled grimly, his eyes resting thoughtfully on Ned. He said nothing for a little while, then murmured something to Dr Leone. The alchemist's eyes widened briefly; then he recovered himself.

'The Count asks if in fact Master Ashby wasn't looking for a lost girl.'

Silence. Three pairs of eyes stared at the Count. But the tawny eyes stared back only into Ned's eyes, unblinkingly. Ned didn't know what to say. The Count murmured something else.

Dr Leone bit his lip. He whispered, 'He asks if you might take a commission from him.'

Ned swallowed. 'A commission? I don't understand.' He felt frightened. What was the Count playing at? What should he do? He looked pleadingly at Dr Leone, who nodded imperceptibly. The meaning in his eyes was clear. *Don't worry. I'll deal with this.*

The alchemist turned to the Count and spoke. The Count answered briefly. Dr Leone translated. 'I said you would be honoured, but first you must find your master. He said that he would try and help you. Give him a description of the assailants.'

Ned stammered, 'I . . . I only really saw the man in the alley, the . . . the one who was pretending to be the Captain. He . . . er . . . he was tall, broad-shouldered, and had the bearing of a man-at-arms. And he—'

He broke off suddenly as the door crashed open. A woman stood framed in the doorway, flanked by a grizzled, burly officer of the guard. She was in her late thirties, quite short, and slim as a whippet, with sharp blue eyes, sallow skin, and silky fair hair teased into an unbecoming style. She was dressed in a brown-and-yellow silk gown that for all its splendour did nothing for her. But it was her air of command which made it quite clear who she was. The Countess of Montemoro!

The Countess spoke. Her first words were in Italian, to the Count. Ned didn't need to understand a word of the language to know she was berating him in no uncertain terms. The Count visibly shrank in his chair as her tirade went on. Meanwhile, the grizzled officer watched with a sardonic curl of the lip. It was plain what he thought of the Count's meekness.

Presently the woman stopped. She turned to Ned and snapped in perfect English, 'I am the Countess of Montemoro. What is the meaning of this intrusion?'

'My . . . my master, my lady,' stammered Ned. 'He's disappeared. Kidnapped by pirates. Dr Leone told us that the Count might be able to help us.'

'Kidnapped by pirates?' Her voice was like a whip. 'On land? I haven't heard of such an event for years.' She turned to the officer. 'Have you, Maffei?'

'No, my lady,' said the man, his impassive glance watching the visitors' faces.

'That's why we came to Venice,' said Ned. 'I mean, not to be kidnapped by pirates,' he hurried on, 'but to investigate some problems my master's ships, and those of his fellow London merchants, have been experiencing lately, due to the depredations of pirates off the coast of Venice.'

The Countess's eyes narrowed. 'Really? Has he spoken to the Council of Ten about it?'

'Not yet, my lady, but—'

'But nothing. I have not heard anyone was here on an official investigative mission.'

'He was trying to do it discreetly,' said Ned.

'I don't think you're telling the truth, boy. Why are you really here?'

'My lady,' said Dr Leone carefully, 'I can assure you that this is a real situation and we—'

'Be quiet, alchemist,' she snapped. 'I was asking the boy a question. Let him answer.' Her blue eyes gimletted Ned's face, as if trying to burrow into his very soul and see the truth there.

'I—I assure you, my lady,' he faltered, 'it's absolutely true. My master has been kidnapped by a gang in Bosco Alley.'

'Why was he in the Bosco Alley?' said the Countess.

'He was to meet an informant. About the piracy business.'

She snorted. 'Then your master is a fool. That area is dangerous. And how could he trust an informant he hadn't even met—and on such a matter too?'

'I . . . I don't know, my lady.'

'Your master must be mad, then. Even if the story you tell is true and you have not come here to spy on us, we cannot help you. You will have to deal with it yourselves.'

'But, my lady, the Count said—'

'You have presumed too much,' said the Countess, moving to her husband's side and placing a hand on his shoulder. Ned distinctly saw the man twitch. 'My husband is not quite himself at present. He should not be bothered with such matters. They should be left to the proper authorities. Go—and do not return.'

'But, sir,' said Dr Leone, turning to the Count, 'you did say you would—'

Montemoro looked away. He waved a hand in dismissal.

'You see?' said the Countess, her eyes gleaming. 'My husband wishes you to go. You have trespassed on his good nature. Too many people do so. I have to constantly watch out for that.'

'Forgive us, my lady,' said Dr Leone coolly. 'We only thought to ask for your husband's advice. But we see now it was a mistake. We will go elsewhere. To the Duke.' His eyes met hers.

She shrugged. 'Then do so. You're such a good friend of his, aren't you, Dr Leone? I'm sure he'll be able to help you. That's what you should have done in the first place. Now be off. You have wasted enough of our time.' She turned to the officer. 'Maffei, kindly have our visitors escorted off the premises.'

And there was nothing any of them could do about it.

As they drew away from the palace, Henri said fiercely, 'We should have told that harridan what we thought of her!'

'What good would that have done?' said Dr Leone. 'She's obviously the true master in that place.'

'It's not just that. I think the Count is actually *afraid* of her,' said Ned.

'Yes. But why?'

Ned had been pondering that. 'Because of the girl. Sarah Tedeschi. You heard what he wanted from me. I think that the commission he wanted to give us was to find her.'

'Yes, I think that too,' said Dr Leone.

'So it must be true, then,' said Ned slowly. 'He's in love with the girl and he's frightened his wife will find out where she is. But he can't know where Sarah is either, or he wouldn't have asked us what he did.'

'Exactly.'

'She spoke almost as though her husband were not competent,' said Henri. 'I mean, as if he were mad.'

'She did. But he's no more mad than you or I, though I'd say he's at the breaking point over something,' said Dr Leone. 'She has some sort of hold over him and he's too afraid to act openly against her.'

'She was listening at the door,' said Ned.

'Yes—she or one of her guards,' said Dr Leone.

'Do you think she heard him talk about the girl and the commission?' said Ned. 'He was speaking fairly softly, but . . .'

'I'm afraid we have to assume she did hear,' said Dr Leone. 'And she interrupted you just as you were describing the attacker—before I had time to translate to the Count what you'd said. And of course she understands English well.' He paused and looked searchingly at Ned. 'You're the only witness who can testify to that man. You're a marked man, Ned. You must leave Venice.'

Ned stared at him in dismay. 'Leave Venice! No! I think I should accept the Count's commission to—'

'Don't be a fool, Ned,' said Dr Leone sharply. 'That's dead in the water, now. You'll never get near him again, she'll make quite sure of that. You're in serious danger, Ned.'

'Ned could hide with us, at our place; she doesn't know where it—' began Henri, but Dr Leone shook his head.

'She'll find out. She will find him there. I think you are safe enough, Henri—you only know the house where Mateo was taken, and I daresay that was only a place of convenience—but Ned has actually seen one of the attackers and can describe him.'

'But I only managed to say he was tall and broad, with the bearing of a man-at-arms!'

'That's enough. Likely enough it was one of her guards, you see. She couldn't let you continue.'

Ned tried once more. 'But the Count—he could help us. . . . I think he wants to.'

'What good does that do? The man is a shivering jelly. Most likely now he'll be locked up and constantly watched.'

Ned was horrified. 'But, sir, she can't do that! He's the Count!'

'But he's not in charge. You saw that clearly, Ned. No. You cannot stay here. Now, I own a small house deep in the countryside in terra firma, the mainland. I am certain the Countess knows nothing of it. In fact, I am sure few do—I use it as a bolt-hole when I'm tired of Venice. I have two or three good staff there, who will look after you. You will be safe there. You must go there today. Right now, without wasting a moment.'

'But, Dr Leone—the others . . . they'll wonder what I—'

'Don't you worry. I'll tell Mistress Quickly.' He smiled. 'And Miss Celia, of course. In fact, I'll make arrangements for them to go there too, a little later. No,' he said when Ned opened his mouth, 'don't argue. Just do as you're told.'

'But what are *you* going to do, sir?' cried Ned.

'I am going to try and get to the bottom of this. Don't worry. I will be careful. And I can defend myself—I'm not unhandy with a sword. What's more, I have powerful friends—and the Countess knows that. That is why I mentioned the Duke.' He smiled faintly. 'I'm not afraid of that hell-harpy. And she knows it. People like her work on the fear of others. And she knows I'm not afraid.' He paused. 'But oddly enough, *she* must be afraid—of her husband going to pieces, and also of Sarah. That's why she's seeking her and why she was prepared to kidnap Mateo. I don't think we're dealing with a simple case of witchcraft or even—sorry, Ned—an unsuitable love affair. Something is very rotten indeed in the Montemoro household—and I intend to find out just what.'

'But what do you think it could be, sir, if it's not that the Count's in love with her?' asked Ned.

'I don't know,' said Dr Leone. 'But my instinct tells me it must be something very serious—perhaps something Sarah witnessed when she was alone in the room with the Count. Or something he told her, perhaps.'

'I can help you in this, sir,' said Henri. 'My father has his own contacts here, including some who know the Montemoro family quite well. I might be of use to you.'

'Very well. If you're careful, then. But you must be prepared to follow what I say and not to question it. Do you understand?'

'Yes, sir. I do.'

'Wait a moment,' said Ned, miffed. 'This isn't fair. Why should Henri be able to stay here and investigate, while I have to cool my heels on the mainland? He's involved too.'

'No. He's *not* involved like you, Ned. He's only known about your mission since last night. And he hasn't been going around questioning people in Cannaregio or the Ghetto, like you have—and believe me, if that hasn't got back to the Countess yet, it soon will. If it *is* she who holds Mateo, then she'll realize now that the man she's holding is connected to you and she will know for sure what you're looking for. And, forgive me, but Jacques d'Arcy and his family are quite well known here, unlike you. Abducting or harming Monsieur d'Arcy's son would be a very serious matter, whereas you—well, you can be written off as just another disposable English spy who poked his nose in where he shouldn't have. Besides, Ned, it's safer for Celia too this way,' Dr Leone added rather cunningly. 'You wouldn't want her put in more danger than necessary, would you?'

Ned flushed. Was he as transparent as all that? He said defiantly, 'I would protect Celia with my life, if need be. But I don't think you quite understand, about her. She is very brave and resourceful. That's why I wanted her to—'

'The house also happens to be in a most idyllic spot,' interrupted Dr Leone gently. 'Arqua, in the Euganean hills. Celia will love it—it was once the house of our great poet, Petrarch. At this time of year, it will be most charming, a real spot for two lovebirds. Flowers, vineyards, olive groves . . .'

'It sounds beautiful,' said Ned, biting his lip. 'But we're not lovebirds. That is, Celia—'

'Just doesn't know her own mind yet,' said Dr Leone calmly. 'Isn't that right, Henri?'

The young Frenchman raised his eyebrows. 'I really would not know,' he said lightly. Suddenly Ned remembered the aborted duel, the hot words between them on the ship. Was Henri glad to be rid of him? Would he and Celia . . .

But before Ned could say anything, Dr Leone, who had been watching the two young men, broke in.

'Look, Ned. I promise to let you know what's happening, as soon as anything does.'

'Hmm,' said Ned doubtfully.

'We will go and hire a suitable boat to take you across to the mainland,' said the alchemist briskly. 'Once there, you will hire a horse to take you to Arqua. Then I will arrange for Celia and Mistress Quickly to join you, at once. Henri, meanwhile, will stay with me. All the time,' he added, with a twinkle in his eye. 'Eh, Henri?'

'Of course,' said Henri smoothly.

'Are you agreed, then, Ned?'

'Oh, very well,' said Ned rather ungraciously. He'd had an idea. He might have to look as though he was heading for the Arqua house, but what was to stop him, once he was left alone, from turning back to Venice?

The three of them fell silent now, as Dr Leone concentrated on steering the gondola through the thickening press of craft on the canal. But if any of them had chanced to look more closely, they might have seen a boat sheltering in the shadow of a landing-stage, where it had been waiting for a few minutes. They might have wondered what the gondolier was waiting for and might then have made out two familiar figures in the passengers who huddled under enveloping blue and green cloaks. They might then have wondered why Celia and Mistress Quickly were apparently hiding from them. But, preoccupied with their troubled thoughts, the men failed to notice anything at all.

Conspiracy

'But, Celia, we should have hailed them!' Mistress Quickly was annoyed. 'You have foolish fancies sometimes!'

'Sorry, Aunt Bess—I couldn't let them see us.'

'But why not?' said her aunt rather peevishly.

'I didn't want them to spoil our little outing,' lied Celia shamelessly. 'Men always want to direct operations and tell you what to look at.'

'That's true enough,' said Mistress Quickly, a little

appeased. 'But you did not need to make quite such a mystery of it.'

Celia ignored that. 'Aunt Bess, did you see who was with them?'

'Yes. Young Henri d'Arcy. Which reminds me, we are expected at the d'Arcy house for dinner tomorrow night.'

'Mmm,' said Celia vaguely. 'Why do you think Henri was with them?'

Bess Quickly stared. 'How should I know?' Her eyes narrowed. 'Do you have a soft spot for that French boy?'

Celia looked back at her boldly. 'No. I don't. He's amusing, but far too fond of himself. Not like his father,' she added mischievously, and was pleased to see the sudden flush that rose to her aunt's cheeks. 'I just want to know what Henri's doing,' she went on. 'What Ned's doing. Why they're as thick as thieves, all of a sudden, when they couldn't stand the sight of each other on the ship.'

'Matthew wasn't with them,' said Mistress Quickly. 'I wonder where he is?'

Off on some trail of his own, Celia thought, even more bitterly. Well, she'd show them, hiding things from her like this!

She turned to the gondolier, who was patiently waiting for his passengers to make up their minds where they wanted to go.

'What houses are further down the canal?' she said, pointing in the direction Dr Leone's gondola had come from.

He smiled, showing broken teeth. 'Many nice palaces, lady. That of the Persico and the Barbarigo and the Montemoro and—'

'Montemoro, you say?' said Celia sharply.

'Yes. That is so. Ca' Montemoro—Montemoro House. Very beautiful house. Very rich family.' He looked sideways at Celia and Mistress Quickly, showing rotten teeth in a sly smile. 'The Montemoros have a wolf on their shield, and it's said the Count was once a wolf to the ladies, but has been tamed by his wife. They do say that the woman there is the lord, not the man.'

'Oh,' said Celia, not really listening to this gossip. So that was where the men had gone! Of course. It made sense. But Master Ashby wasn't with them. So most likely, he had either stayed behind, at Ca' Montemoro, or gone ahead somewhere else. The other three had been heading back towards Dr Leone's district when Celia and Mistress Quickly had seen them. And going quite rapidly too. Getting back before Celia and Mistress Quickly noticed they'd gone?

'Would you like to look more closely at the Montemoro palace, *signorina*?' said the gondolier, interrupting her thoughts.

Celia was about to say yes, when she saw the speculative expression on his face. She shook her head.

'I don't think so,' she said casually. 'My aunt and I, we wish to see the Ca' d'Oro—the Golden House.'

'Oh, of course,' said the gondolier with a broad smile. 'Ladies, they always like the Golden House. It is a good choice. We go now?'

'Yes,' said Celia calmly. She turned to Mistress Quickly. 'He is taking us to see the Golden House,' she said.

'Did I hear him say something about those Montemoros?' said Mistress Quickly, settling herself comfortably on the cushions.

'Yes. He was saying they were unpleasant people.'

'Ten to one, that's where Orlan— Dr Leone and the others were coming from.'

Celia shrugged and tried to look indifferent. 'I suppose so. But who cares, on such a fine morning?'

'I'm glad to hear you say that, child,' said Mistress Quickly. 'I don't like the unsuitable way you've been dragged into this ugly business. I'm glad you've seen sense.'

'Yes, Aunt Bess,' said Celia meekly.

They set off again, in the opposite direction to the Montemoro palace, passing under the Rialto bridge and the famous markets clustered around it. They duly oohed and aahed over Ca' d'Oro, a fantastic gilded palace of Gothic grandeur, and sailed slowly past many other grand palaces, too many to remember. Then, on Celia's instructions, the gondolier turned into the

Cannaregio canal and tied up his boat at a landing-stage a little distance from the entrance.

'There's something I thought you'd like, Aunt Bess,' said Celia, to forestall any questions from Mistress Quickly. 'Ned and I saw a rather lovely little shop here yesterday—it has the finest selections of ribbons and combs I've ever seen.'

That was perfectly true. Casting around for some excuse to stop here, she'd remembered that the day before she had seen the shop, which was not very far from the bridge that led to the Ghetto. She'd noticed it because even at the time she'd thought Aunt Bess would love it. If she could get her aunt ensconced in there for a little while, she might just have time to slip across and find Dr Tedeschi without Mistress Quickly being any the wiser.

Mistress Quickly was quite unsuspecting of any underhanded motive. She clapped her hands with pleasure. 'What a good idea! You are a dear girl, Celia, and most thoughtful!'

Celia felt a little mean then. But that soon faded as Bess Quickly waddled through the door of the shop and plunged herself into the atmosphere she so loved. It was a good deed Celia had just done, and not a trick at all. Watching her aunt bent over a whole selection of silken ribbons, her face flushed, her eyes sparkling, Celia thought she would be there for quite a while, happy as a hen in a dust bath. The time would come when she would want to make some purchases and then Celia would have to help her. But for the moment, she could be safely left to her own devices. Muttering a few words to the effect that she would soon be back, Celia slipped out of the shop, down the street, and over the bridge, into the Ghetto.

Celia had a very good sense of orientation once she'd been to a place, and she remembered the layout of the streets very well. Here was the house where they'd spoken to the little boy; he was not to be seen today. He'd said Dr Tedeschi's house was in the next street, and turning the corner, Celia soon saw which house it must be. There was a sign creaking above a door, painted with the international symbol of the doctor: a wooden staff with a snake curled around it.

Taking no notice of the curious glances of a couple of passersby, she went up to the house and knocked at the door. It was opened almost immediately by a plainly dressed dark woman of about thirty-five, with a pair of very fine black eyes. Eyes that glared suspiciously at Celia.

'Who are you? What do you want?' Her Italian was harshly accented with German intonations.

Celia thought: *This must be Jacob Tedeschi's sister. The one Dr Leone said was a bit of a tartar*. She smiled winningly. 'This is the doctor's house, no? Dr Tedeschi?'

The woman looked at her with even more suspicion. 'Who wants to know?' She added, 'He doesn't deal with hussies and their problems. You'll have to go to another doctor for that.'

'I'm not a hussy, signora,' said Celia, flushing. 'I'm English.'

The woman snorted. 'Ha! And that is supposed to make you *not* a hussy?' Then she frowned. 'I am not signora, but signorina. I have never married. Men are an unreliable lot. And how is it you speak such good Italian, anyway?'

'Because I learned to,' said Celia. 'Please, signorina, can you go and get Dr Tedeschi? Tell him it's important. It's about Sarah.'

The woman's face froze. She stared at Celia.

'Please, I'm a friend. My father came to see him yesterday. Master Matthew Ashby.'

The woman's face cleared. 'Ah, the one from England sent to us by Baptista Bassano's daughter. So. You are this man's daughter. And so?'

'I need to speak to Dr Tedeschi,' said Celia, exasperated.

'What for? You have found Sarah?'

'No, but—'

'My brother Jacob is a busy man,' said the woman. 'I will not disturb him for a "no, but."'

'Please, Signorina Tedeschi, will you find out if he might see me, just for a minute or two? My father has sent me to ask a very important question. It could mean the difference between finding Sarah and—'

'Not finding her,' said the woman crossly. 'What is your name, girl?'

'Celia Ashby.'

'Very well, Celia Ashby. I am Rachel Tedeschi. Come into the waiting room. There are no patients here at the moment. Sit here. Don't move. I will go and see if my brother has time enough to speak to you.'

'Thank you, signorina,' said Celia very politely. As Rachel marched briskly away, Celia smiled to herself. The doctor must not get too many frivolous-minded visitors with this dragon guarding the gate!

A short time later, the dragon-lady came back, followed by a tall, bespectacled man with thin greying dark hair, a small beard, and a gentle smile. 'Miss Ashby, thank you for coming.' He spoke a passable English, if a little hesitant.

'I can speak Italian, if you prefer, Doctor,' said Celia.

Dr Tedeschi said, 'Very well, if that does not bother you. Rachel, perhaps we might have a warm drink and a cake?'

'Please, Dr Tedeschi, that won't be necessary,' said Celia hurriedly, envisaging hours of ritual politeness—and Aunt Bess at last tiring of the ribbon shop and looking around for her. 'I will only use a few minutes of your time. My father asked me to check something for him.'

'Ah. I understand. He is on the track of something?' The doctor's eyes lit up with hope.

Celia swallowed. 'Yes. That is so. This is the question

he asked me to put to you: what was the room like, where your patient lay?'

Dr Tedeschi and his sister looked startled. The doctor said, 'I am sorry, signorina, but I do not understand.'

'The room, where the patient lay. Where Sarah watched him, when you went out to mix your medicines. Where was it, in the Montemoro mansion?'

'A bedroom on the second floor. There was an arched window looking over the canal, I fancy . . . the door into the room from the corridor outside . . . and another door in the room.'

'Where did that door lead?'

'To a storeroom, I believe. I didn't go in there.'

'Did the Count come in through the door from the corridor?'

Dr Tedeschi stared at her. 'I presume so. Sarah said he only came in briefly, to check on the patient's condition. She exchanged maybe two, three sentences with him, that's all. Then he left. Sarah was only alone with him for a couple of minutes, nothing more.' Dr Tedeschi sounded defensive.

'Where did you go, Doctor, when you went to prepare your mixtures?'

'Your father asked me that yesterday,' said Dr Tedeschi. 'Surely you don't need—'

'Just to check, Doctor. Please.'

'A small room downstairs, where herbs are kept.'

'Did you see anyone on the way up or down? The Count—anyone?'

'No. But that isn't surprising.'

'Dr Tedeschi, who was the patient?'

His face darkened. 'I have answered this question too.'

'What for are you repeating and repeating?' said Rachel. 'My brother is a busy man and cannot be asked to go over things again and again.'

'Please, Doctor. There is a good reason for this, I assure you,' said Celia desperately.

His thoughtful gaze rested on her. 'Very well. The patient is called Lucia Gardi. She's a companion of the Countess. A distant relative, I believe. She was very ill, poor soul. Stomach cramps, vomiting.'

'Is she pretty?'

This time he stared frankly at her. 'Pretty? What an odd question, signorina. No. She's not pretty. She's a good deal older than the Countess. A mousy kind of lady. Meek, you know.'

'Hag-ridden by the Montemoro woman, I should think,' said his sister tartly.

'Rachel, please, be charitable.'

Rachel's eyes flashed. 'About that monster? Are you crazy, Jacob?' She shook her head and said to Celia, 'My brother—he's too good to live.'

'It's just that nothing is served by insulting her, even in private,' said the doctor wearily. 'It is not revenge

I seek—it is my Sarah back and an end to this matter. I cannot understand why it has happened. The Countess knows my Sarah is no witch.'

'Of course she does,' said Celia eagerly. 'That's not why she's hunting her, Doctor, don't you see? It's my—my father's belief that in fact the Countess thinks that your daughter Sarah saw something that night, when you went to treat your patient at the Montemoro house. She thinks that Sarah might have witnessed something.'

'So that's why you asked those questions,' said the doctor. 'I see. Well, Sarah did talk of a conspiracy in the note she left me when she vanished, but I did not really take heed of it, you understand. I just thought she was afraid and uncomprehending, as I was, and seeking answers, even absurd ones. But now—what you say, it makes sense. Yes.'

'But what could our Sarah have seen?' exclaimed Rachel. 'What dreadful deed, to make this woman accuse her of this wicked thing? And why talk of the Count?'

'I don't know. But it must be a clue,' said Celia, thinking out loud. 'It must have something to do with the Count, in that room. What did he do?'

'Looked in at the patient.'

'Did he say anything?'

'Very little, from what I understand. Just small talk. But you see, I never had the chance to discuss it with Sarah before she vanished. It all happened so quickly.'

'I see. Do you know how long he was in the room?'

'Less than two or three minutes; then a guard came in. The Count left, then, before I came back.'

'And in the time he was alone with her, he did not try to touch Sarah or make any—any improper advances to her?'

His eyes flashed. 'No. Nothing of the sort. I would have understood what was behind the Countess's accusation, if that was so. But Sarah swore nothing like that had happened.'

'Oh,' said Celia. She thought a bit. 'Did Sarah meet the Countess?'

'No. She did not look in to see the patient at all.'

'Did she meet her another day? Perhaps when the Countess accused Sarah?'

'Do you really think such as she would come here, to the Ghetto, to deliver her message?' broke in Rachel Tedeschi scornfully. 'She sent one of her servants.'

'So the accusation came in a message?'

'Yes. Not a written message, though,' said Dr Tedeschi. 'A verbal one.' His face darkened. 'I blame myself. I was not there that morning. I was visiting a patient in the Ghetto and my sister was at the market. Sarah was alone. She did not tell us what had happened. And that night she disappeared, leaving the note in which she explained and said she believed there was a conspiracy and she was an innocent victim of it. Well, I immediately went to see our neighbour and he said that yes, a messenger in the

Montemoro livery had come and knocked on the door and Sarah had answered it. I did not let on what it was about, because of what Sarah had said in her note, but I let it be known that it was just about a follow-up visit to Signora Gardi. You have to be careful with neighbours gossiping.'

'Can I see Sarah's note, Dr Tedeschi?'

'I destroyed it. Sarah asked me to.'

'I wish you hadn't,' said his sister, snorting a little. 'It would have been good evidence.'

'She said it was too dangerous,' said the doctor. 'She said I must not worry and that above all I must not try and reason with the Montemoros, that I must pretend to be completely ignorant of what had happened, even of the accusation itself. She also said I must not try and find her or send anyone to look for her. But how could I just sit there and wait for news? I determined that I would seek help—but from far away, where it couldn't be connected to us.'

'Ah,' said Celia. 'That's just what I thought. The Countess was trying to frighten Sarah. She didn't have any real evidence against her. Otherwise why not just take it to the authorities? She was afraid Sarah knew something—had seen or heard something, that day at the palace. . . . Dr Tedeschi, I heard the patient recovered.'

'Yes, she did recover. Though her health is not good, generally.'

Celia's eyes glittered. 'Dr Tedeschi, could the patient . . . could Signora Gardi have been *poisoned*?'

He looked quickly at her. 'You mean, because of her symptoms? I did give her a purgative, but there was no real reason to suspect poison. In any case, why would anyone want to poison this insignificant soul? And if it is this which the Countess was afraid of us suspecting, why wouldn't she go after *me,* too? In fact, why call me in, in the first place?'

'That's true,' said Celia, deflated. 'You're right. It can't be anything to do with this Signora Gardi. It must be something else, something Sarah witnessed, something whose importance she perhaps did not realize at the time. Oh! I wish I could speak to her!'

Too late, she realized what she'd said. She went crimson. 'Oh, I'm so sorry, Dr Tedeschi, signorina. Please forgive me. I really didn't mean . . .'

'I understand,' the doctor said heavily. 'You are young, and this is exciting for you, a chase, a mystery. It is different for us.'

'Yes. Of course. Please forgive me,' said poor Celia, feeling twice as embarrassed now.

'Yet you are right. We too, we'd also like to speak to her,' said the doctor with a gentle smile. 'We'd like to tell her to get away, run as far as she can from Venice and never come back. For if it is truly a dangerous conspiracy that she has unwittingly stumbled into, then her life is in even more danger than if it were a charge of witchcraft, which I think we could disprove.' He looked at Celia. 'Tell your father that I think he is right—that Sarah must have witnessed something that night which has put her life in danger.' His eyes were suddenly bright, as if from unshed tears. 'My poor girl—she tries to be so brave, to shield us. But she is rash and stubborn. I wish she had not done this. I wish I had known earlier. I could have helped her.'

'We could have helped her together,' said Rachel, sniffing. 'I am a woman. She could have talked to me about it. But Sarah is headstrong.'

'Almost as much as you, Rachel,' said her brother, smiling faintly. He took a deep breath. 'But I am truly glad we have found honest, good people to help us.' He turned to Celia. 'Tell your father. Tell him.'

'I will,' said Celia a little uncomfortably. 'Thank you, Dr Tedeschi. You have been most helpful.'

At that moment, there came a knock on the door.

'Fuss, fuss, fuss, it never stops,' said Rachel, and went to answer the door. Celia chose that moment to say goodbye to Dr Tedeschi and promise she'd come back as soon as there was any news. As she crossed the hall to go, however, the Tedeschis' visitor came in, with a most unhappy-looking Rachel behind him. 'Forgive me, Jacob,' she said, 'I tried to stop him, but he just pushed his way in, unmannerly creature that he is.'

The newcomer was a large man in more ways than one—tall and fat and richly dressed. But he looked nothing like the jolly fat man of legend—there was a sharpness in his hazel eyes and a tension in his jowly face that put Celia in mind rather of a prowling cat. He said, without preamble, 'I know your daughter's run off with her fancy man, Tedeschi. Don't even try to argue. I have proof of it.'

'Proof? Proof? There is no proof of anything. You are not welcome in this house, Solomon Tartuffo, and you can get out of it this minute.' Dr Tedeschi was like a man transformed, the gentle eyes flashing, the stooped frame straightening.

The merchant snorted. 'Ha! Of course I am not welcome. No good Jew is welcome. Only riffraff and Gentiles.' His eyes flicked over Celia contemptuously. 'In some cases, both together.'

'How dare you insult our guests!' Jacob Tedeschi advanced on the visitor like an avenging angel. His very hair seemed to crackle with anger. 'You will leave, this instant.'

'Not till I tell you what I have come to say. I know who your daughter's lover is.' He smiled nastily. 'And it is not even a rich man she is throwing her religion and customs away for, so you need not think you will get any advantage from it, Jacob. It is riffraff. Pure riffraff. And I have proof of it; living proof.'

At that, Rachel Tedeschi gave a great cry and threw herself at Tartuffo, beating at him with her fists. 'Liar!

Liar!' she yelled. 'Wicked liar! God will punish you for your wicked, wicked lies!'

'Rachel! Don't!' Dr Tedeschi pulled her back. 'He's not worth it.' Holding her, he said tightly to Tartuffo, 'If you have proof, Solomon, produce it.'

For answer, Tartuffo gave a whistle. And into the house came a man whom Celia recognized at once. It was the wolfish man from Cannaregio!

MURANO

Dr Leone soon found a boatman who would take Ned to the mainland within half an hour. There wasn't enough time for Ned to go back to Dr Leone's house, so the alchemist gave him some money for the boat trip, the horse at the other end, and some food. After making Ned solemnly swear that he'd leave Venice, he rowed away with Henri. It was clear he had thought of some line of enquiry and was determined to go and pursue it at once, unencumbered by Ned.

Left alone, Ned paced around the quay, waiting for the

boatman to be ready and too annoyed to even think about eating. He wished he hadn't sworn to go. Every instinct told him he shouldn't. After all, Master Ashby was his master, Celia's father, and Mistress Quickly's brother; Dr Leone was only Master Ashby's friend. It wasn't right to run away when his master was in danger. *I must think of something—and fast,* thought Ned.

The quay was crowded with sailors and porters, who were much too busy to pay any attention to him. He wandered amongst them, trying to think of a plan. Could he perhaps go and come back almost at once? Dr Leone hadn't said anything about that; he'd just made Ned promise to go. If Ned did that, though, he couldn't go back to the alchemist's house, or to Henri's. He'd have to hide somewhere. And he didn't have enough money to rent a room. He turned out his pockets and looked at all the money he had, including what Dr Leone had given him. He judged he had enough to survive for a few days, anyway, if he was very careful and slept in doorways or under bridges. His heart raced. He'd never done this before. He'd always had a roof over his head. But it seemed the right thing to do.

Yes, he thought excitedly. *That's exactly what I'll do. I'll leave Venice—that is, I'll get the boatman to take me not to the mainland, but to the closest island in the lagoon—Murano, isn't it? You can see it from Cannaregio's northern quays. Then I'll get a Murano boatman to take me back to Cannaregio. That won't cost much. . . . And I can hide somewhere in that district, and try to somehow speak to the Count on his own. How, I don't know. But I have to try, at least.*

At first, the boatman was a little surprised that Ned wanted to go to Murano and not the mainland, but when Ned explained, with lots of gestures, that he'd be paid exactly the same, he brightened. It was obviously rather more than a trip to Murano was worth.

They reached Murano very quickly and Ned tipped the boatman an extra coin, putting a finger to his lips as he did so. '*Ragazza,*' he said, remembering the word for 'girl,' and the stories he'd heard of Venetian gallantry, and hoping the boatman would get the message that he'd sneaked off to meet a girl in Murano.

The boatman laughed and winked. '*Si, si, signore,*' he said approvingly. He went off, shaking his head over the antics of the young, and Ned breathed a sigh of relief. Good. Now he could wait here a few minutes and spend a little more money in getting back. But no need for generosity this time. He'd just pay the basic price.

To pass the time, he looked around him. Murano seemed quite as busy as Venice, and as crowded. It was also almost as rich, with magnificent palaces and churches. Its wealth rested on the delicate, expensive product it was famous for: glass. Murano was the greatest glass-producer in the whole of Europe and had been so for centuries. So jealously did it guard that fame that, though its glass-makers were well paid and cossetted, they could not leave Murano to found glass-making businesses elsewhere—on pain of death!

Ned was looking in at a glass-blower's stall, admiring a set of glasses with a good many other gawkers, when suddenly he stiffened. He'd briefly seen someone reflected in the wares of the glass-maker. That stance—it was familiar. Surely it couldn't be . . . He looked again. And at that moment, the man turned his head and Ned saw the other side of his face. It was a hard face, though younger than he'd imagined—*and its left cheek was bisected by a long, livid scar.*

Ned bent down quickly, as if he'd dropped something. The last thing he wanted was for the man to see him. He'd probably had a better look at Ned than the reverse. It wouldn't do at all for the man to see him. Unless, thought Ned, with a lurch of the heart, unless he followed me, to deal with me. But he thrust the thought away almost immediately. The man hadn't seen him. And he might lead Ned to where Dr Ashby was being held. *I have to know for sure,* thought Ned.

He dared a glance up. The scarred man was talking to the glass-maker. He had his back to Ned. Now was the time to make himself scarce. Ned scuttled away without being challenged and hid around the corner. He stayed there and watched as the glass-maker and the scarred man talked for a few more seconds. Then the scarred man put a hand on the glass-maker's shoulder and left. Waiting an instant longer, Ned sauntered casually after him, taking care not to look as if he was following, but stopping now and then at some other glass-maker's shop or other such thing. Nobody took any notice of him. Clearly, they were used to gawkers.

The scarred man walked rapidly into the maze of little streets that led into the heart of the city. He crossed a bridge and came to a house on the other side. There he stopped, rapped on the door, was let in, and disappeared through the doorway.

Ned's heart raced. This must be where they were keeping Master Ashby. He must get in! He looked speculatively up at the house. Like most houses here, it was three storeys high, with a barred window on the bottom floor and two narrow windows and a carved stone balcony on the first floor. If he could climb up to the balcony he might be able to get in. But he couldn't play the monkey in broad daylight; someone might see him and raise the alarm. He'd have to wait till nightfall. It was early afternoon now. He stood indecisively for a moment. Should he wait here and try to get into the house? Or should he go back to Venice and try to get into the Montemoro palace? No, on balance, it seemed more likely he'd get into this place—where nobody knew he was around—than into the palace, where it was quite possible the Countess might be expecting him to try and come back in secret.

So he went slowly back to the bridge. There was a space just under it, from where he could watch the house without being seen. He was feeling quite hungry now, but he didn't dare leave his post, in case anything happened at the house—say, if the scarred man reappeared.

BETRAYAL

Celia hung back a little. Would the wolfish man recognize her as the urchin who had asked him all those questions about Jewish girls the day before? It was unlikely, but she couldn't be sure. Part of her wanted to flee; part of her wanted to stay, to hear what the man had to say. And she was stricken with pity for the Tedeschis, who looked as though the sky was falling in on them.

Tartuffo was speaking. 'Tell them, Marco, tell them what you heard.'

The wolfish man licked his lips. He shot a look at

Celia and smiled. It was not a smile of recognition, but the predatory smile of the habitual woman-hunter. He said, 'I heard it from the lips of a street urchin, talking about the luck his English friend had with a pretty Jewish girl.'

Celia stiffened and stared at Marco.

'This is your proof?' said Dr Tedeschi coldly. His clenched face relaxed. 'This man and his hearsay? His vicious gossip? Go, Solomon, go—and take your informer with you. We have heard enough.'

'You have not heard it all,' said Tartuffo just as coldly. 'Go on, Marco. Tell them.'

'The boy told me his English friend, who was a young soldier of fortune, had managed to tumble this Jewish girl. Said she was very lovely and that she was the only daughter of a Ghetto doctor, who was blind as a bat and didn't see what was going on under his nose. He had first clapped eyes on her because . . . er . . . because he and his friends had come to visit the doctor. For treatment, you understand. He implied that it was for the sort of illness that is common amongst those who earn their living by the sword.' He shuffled his feet, pretending to be shy. 'Unmentionable diseases.'

'Ha!' Tartuffo sneered. 'When I think my son—a good, solid boy—was not good enough for your Sarah! You looked down your long nose at us, Jacob, because we didn't have your intellectual pretensions and your connections out there! Well, there's an end to it now!

When everyone knows that your daughter is no more than a soldier's whore, they'll—'

'Get out!' whispered Dr Tedeschi. 'Get out.'

'I'll go when I'm good and ready,' said Tartuffo calmly. 'You are finished here—you, your tartar of a sister, and your whore of a daughter. I came here to give you a chance to prove to me that this story cannot be true. And what do I find? You do not even challenge it. You only insult me. That is proof of a kind too.'

'Have you quite finished?' said Dr Tedeschi. He was very pale. 'Does your informer have more to say, or is this the sum total of your charge?'

'That is all I have to say, your honour,' said Marco rather obsequiously. But his eyes, glittering with a nasty pleasure, belied his regretful words. 'I am sorry to have been the source of distress to your family.' He shot another glance at Celia. 'And I am sorry if I have scandalized your visitor.'

'Shut up, Marco,' snapped Tartuffo. 'He's not worth toadying to, can't you see? The man's finished. With this proof, I can go to the rabbi and have them ostracized; and what is more, I can go to the authorities and tell them what has been going on. No decent Jew or Christian wants such scandalous goings-on to be permitted. Jacob, if you think that your daughter's disgrace will be the end of the matter, you had better think again. You will no longer be welcome in Venice. No one, Jew or Gentile, will come near your practice.'

Dr Tedeschi stared at him. 'Why do you hate me so, Solomon?' he said. 'What have I done to you, to deserve this?'

'Don't ask,' snapped Rachel Tedeschi. 'This man is not worth a single breath of yours.'

Tartuffo ignored her. 'Hate you? I don't hate you. I despise you. You, *Doctor,* with your holier-than-thou nose in the air, and your butter-wouldn't-melt daughter and your spinster dragon of a sister. You are frauds, liars, cheats. You don't belong here. You don't belong anywhere. You—'

'You are a wicked man,' said Celia, at last finding her voice. A wild rage boiled in her. 'You are wicked and stupid and ignorant. How dare you speak in this disgusting way, when you know nothing, nothing, nothing!'

Dr Tedeschi made a movement towards her, but Celia took no notice. She advanced on Tartuffo with her head high in the air and her eyes on fire. 'You don't know what's been going on and you take the word of a vicious liar'—and she waved at Marco—'a man who boasts of seducing Jewish girls by the dozen but who is just lying through his teeth. Ask him about the daughter of the moneylender, for instance! You take the word of a predator, of a man who thinks Jews are scum—yes, those were his very words—against one of your own people!'

'How do you know . . . ?' cried Marco, then thought better of what he'd been about to say.

'How do I know? Damned out of your own mouth, aren't you! Well, Marco, I saw you, yesterday, in Cannaregio. I overheard you speaking to an urchin boy and a young foreign gallant. And so I know that he never said anything of the kind to you.'

Marco stared at her and went very pale. She knew he still hadn't recognized her, but that he knew the game was up now. He didn't look wolfish now so much as like a beaten dog. She ignored him and turned back to the merchant. 'Have you ever, *ever* had real cause to believe Sarah was anything other than she should be?'

Tartuffo stared at her. At first he had looked bewildered by her intervention, but now he recovered. 'She was always stuck-up and looked like she knew a secret the rest of us didn't. It's enough to make me suspect there was something else behind that superior manner of hers. And her father let her get away with too much. She was not brought up properly. Why, he even sent her to dancing classes—'

'The very idea!' Celia sneered.

'And he allowed her to read unsuitable books and think unsuitable thoughts.' He looked Celia up and down. 'Besides, I don't care what creatures like Marco think of us—or creatures like you, come to that. And it may be that he is as you describe . . .'

'But, your honour—' protested Marco.

'It was he who came to me with his story,' snapped Tartuffo, ignoring Marco. 'He said he had heard I had been wronged by these people and that he had information that might be of interest to me.'

'Really?' said Celia in a cold voice. She plunged on. 'Is it not convenient indeed? Did you not ask yourself why he should come to you, unasked?' Without waiting for an answer, she wheeled around on Marco. 'Were you sent by the Countess Montemoro to make trouble for the Tedeschis with this man?'

He stared at her. But before he could speak, Tartuffo yelled, 'The Countess Montemoro! What are you raving about? What do the Montemoros have to do with me?'

'Not with you, signore,' said Celia bitingly. 'But with the Tedeschis.'

'No, signorina,' said Dr Tedeschi urgently.

But in her rage Celia threw caution to the wind. 'Listen to me, you fool,' she hissed, leaning towards Tartuffo. 'The Countess Montemoro wants to destroy Sarah because the girl knows something. Something really bad. That is why she had to vanish. Her life is in danger. And you are part of that, you blind, ignorant, wicked fool. The Countess is using you to try and flush Sarah out.'

Tartuffo gazed at her, speechless. His mouth kept opening and closing, but no words came out. But Dr Tedeschi said wearily, 'Oh, child. You should not have spoken so. You should not have said. We could have borne these other things because we know they are not true. But now—now you have put my poor Sarah into even greater danger.'

Celia couldn't answer. The tide of rage that had swept over her was receding, but its impact still beat in her blood, making her scalp tingle.

Tartuffo suddenly found his voice. 'I don't know what you're implying, Jacob, but I tell you I want no part of this. None.'

Dr Tedeschi looked at him. 'No, Solomon? Don't you want to join our enemies the Montemoros? Wouldn't that fit your plan very nicely indeed? Come on, what are you waiting for? Get your fat carcass over to Ca' Montemoro with your toady and tell them what you've heard here. Go on. Do it! Do it!' His voice rose. 'The Countess wants to burn my daughter as a witch. A Jewish witch. Isn't that even juicier than a Jewish whore, Solomon? Come on, you could help to light the fire. And soon, it could be burning down the whole Ghetto, as all the old hatreds are reawoken, and the scum of the city see a chance to take their revenge on the ones they see as the killers of Christ. But you—you would be safe with your new friends the Montemoros, wouldn't you?'

'If you think I . . .' The colour had gone out of Tartuffo's cheeks and he looked grey. 'If you think I want anything to do with a thing like that, you are even madder than I thought.' He paused, then shouted, 'You are a fool, Tedeschi! You can't even manage your own daughter! You make enemies of one of the most powerful families in Venice! You are crazy! Crazy!'

'And you're disgusting, Solomon,' said Dr Tedeschi in

a dead sort of voice. 'You don't even have the courage of your own hatred. Get out of my sight—and don't ever come back.'

And to Celia's surprise Tartuffo did just that. Without another word, without a look behind him, he waddled out of the house. Marco tried to sidle out behind him, but Celia was too quick for him. She flew to the door and slammed it shut, barring the way.

'Oh, no!' she yelled. 'You're not leaving!'

'We'll see about that,' hissed Marco and, quick as a flash, he drew his dagger. He came at Celia, but she ducked and swiftly kicked up, connecting hard with his hand. He yelled with pain, the dagger flew out of his hand, and Celia quickly put her foot on it. She shouted, 'Dr Tedeschi! Grab him!'

But it was Rachel who moved first. Picking up a heavy poker that lay against the wall, she advanced on Marco with a determined look in her eyes. Then her brother moved on him from the other side, pinning the informer between them. When Celia picked up the dagger and came towards him too, it was too much for Marco. He fell on his knees. *No, not a wolf at all,* thought Celia, disgusted. *Just a cringing dog.*

'Please, your honour,' he wheedled. 'I meant no harm. I really didn't. It's hard for a poor man to earn a living, you see, and . . . Please, don't kill me. I'll promise I'll say nothing. Nothing at all.'

'No, indeed you won't,' said Rachel Tedeschi tightly,

and before anyone could react she had brought the poker crashing down on his head. He crumpled and fell to the floor.

'Rachel!' cried Dr Tedeschi in what sounded like real distress. 'You shouldn't have done that. There was no need.'

'Oh, yes, there was,' said his sister grimly. 'I saw his hand move. He was going to snatch the dagger back from Celia. The creature's like a snake and not to be trusted.'

'But you might have killed him!' Dr Tedeschi was on his knees beside Marco. He felt for his pulse.

'But I see by your face that I haven't,' said Rachel calmly. 'We can't leave him like this,' she went on. She seemed to have completely recovered the poise that had so deserted her when Tartuffo had come in. 'He must not be allowed to get away. We will tie him up and put him safely away. And when he wakes up, we can ask him some questions.'

'But, Rachel, I don't want to hold him prisoner,' protested Dr Tedeschi. 'And the Countess may come looking for him.'

'Let her, if she dares,' said his sister fiercely. 'By then, we'll know what she's been up to.'

Dr Tedeschi sighed and gave in to the inevitable. 'Very well, then.'

No sooner said than done: Marco was soon securely trussed up and carried into a small room nearby. It was windowless and, when the door was bolted and locked, impossible to escape from.

Outside the room once more, Dr Tedeschi gave a faint, melancholy smile. 'My dear Signorina Ashby, you got rather more than you bargained for when you came here to deliver a simple message for your father.'

Celia looked into his honest, troubled eyes and found she couldn't lie to him. She said, 'Actually, it was not my father who sent me, Doctor. It was all my own idea. This is how it happened. . . .' And she told them, finishing with: 'And now I'd better get back to my aunt, who—'

'Your aunt is outside?' cut in Rachel Tedeschi. 'Then you must go and fetch her. Whatever will she think of us?'

'She's not outside,' said Celia hurriedly. 'She's in a ribbon shop near the canal—at least, I hope she's still there, and not setting a hue and cry out for me. . . . Still, she knows me and that I tend to disappear sometimes, so I hope she'll just be exploring the other shops and not worry about me too much.' She hesitated, then went on quickly, 'I'm sorry, but I really must tell you. That story Marco told . . .'

'Yes?'

'It was me—I mean, I was the urchin boy and my friend Ned was the supposed soldier of fortune. He's not at all, you know—he's assistant to my father. And my . . . my best friend. The friend of my heart.' She swallowed as the words of truth came out of her mouth, and she thought: *It's true. He is the friend of my heart. He always has been. But it's only now I see it clearly.* 'We . . . we were just trying to find out some information that would help your daughter. I'm sorry. I never thought it could be twisted like this.'

There was a little silence; then Dr Tedeschi said, 'Don't be sorry, signorina. We understand. And that creature—he might have done more good than he could have dreamed.'

'I don't understand. . . .'

Dr Tedeschi's eyes met his sister's. It was she who said slowly, 'You see, my dear, it made us remember something. Someone, that is.'

'Someone who had completely slipped our minds,' said her brother, 'because, well, because it seemed unimportant at the time and they were only here the once. We never saw them again.' He took a deep breath. 'I could not say so in front of those two, of course. But a few months ago, I did treat a sick soldier. He was very ill, though not with the illness referred to. But he was a lost soul; mad, sick in the head, you understand. He came with two friends: soldiers too. They were younger than him, especially one of them. Well, at least they had *been* soldiers, I think; they had lately come home from some war or other.'

'I don't like soldiers,' said Rachel sharply. 'Rough, violent men. The less we see of them here, the better. I said to you then you shouldn't deal with them.'

'The man was in pain; he was raving. I could hardly leave even a dog like that,' said Dr Tedeschi gently. 'His friends explained they'd tried to help him, but could not. They behaved decently while they were here.'

'Did Sarah . . . did she see them?'

'She came in, once, to bring me some medicines. She did not speak to them. One of the soldiers made a remark to her, but she didn't answer. He talked a little to me—inconsequential things. His other friend, however—the youngest one—said nothing at all.'

'What happened to the patient?'

'There is little you can do for such a condition, for it cannot be cured,' sighed the doctor. 'It comes and goes with the moon. But I was able to calm him, give him a sleeping draught, let him rest here for an hour or two. One of his friends—the one who didn't talk—stayed at his bedside, while his comrade went out and came back later.'

'Could Sarah . . . could she have talked to him then?'

There was silence. Then Dr Tedeschi said simply, 'I don't know.' He went on, 'But they left as soon as the patient was awake. He was a little better then. I remember how gentle that comrade of his was with him, how he helped him to the door, supported him. The other did so too, but out of a sense of duty, you felt—not friendship. Or perhaps because he was in awe of the other man—the silent one, I mean.'

'Who were they, Dr Tedeschi?'

'They left no names. They were wary men, you see.' He sighed. 'I don't even know what regiment they may have been in. I know little of such things. And there are many ex-soldiers wandering around, as I'm sure you've seen. They do not find it always easy to get other work when they come home.'

'Well, at least they paid on the nail,' said Rachel Tedeschi tartly. 'Soldiers are often lacking in money, but these paid up without a quibble.'

'That was the only time the silent man spoke,' said Dr Tedeschi. 'He thanked me, said I had done a great kindness for his poor friend, and that he would never forget it.'

'Did Sarah hear that?'

'Yes. I'm sure she did. She was at the door with me. It may well have stayed in her mind. But then there's the other thing that Marco's lie made me remember. That poor madman was, I believe, of your own nationality—or at least could speak some English. In his delirium, he shouted, in that tongue: "Help me, help me, find her. . . ." He also called on a woman's name.'

Celia stared at him as a memory jolted her. 'Do you remember what the woman's name was, Dr Tedeschi?'

He frowned. 'Was it Sylvia? Bella, perhaps. No. No. I remember now. It was *Beatrice*. That's right. Beatrice. I know because it reminded me of the poet Dante and his love for his Beatrice, and I—'

She interrupted him. 'Oh, Dr Tedeschi, I think I know who you're talking about!'

The doctor looked puzzled. 'Beatrice? You know this Beatrice?'

'No, no. The madman! Ned saw him, the first day we arrived in Venice. He spoke to him. I saw him too, yesterday, but only in passing. . . . But I'm going to run and fetch Ned, right now. Please, wait for me. I'll be back as soon as I can.'

'And what of your poor aunt, waiting and waiting?' cried Rachel Tedeschi, but she was speaking to thin air. Celia had already gone.

A SURPRISE

Ned was feeling very fed up. Nothing had happened for the last hour or two. It was deadly boring. He glanced at the quiet house. Perhaps he should try and get in there before nightfall after all. They might well use the darkness—to move Master Ashby, or whatever. *Or whatever* . . . He shivered. If they hadn't got anything out of the old philosopher, then what would they do? They might well just think he'd outlived his usefulness, and . . .

No. He couldn't wait. He must get in. He looked

around. The street was deserted and so was the one on the other side of the bridge. In fact, fewer than ten people had passed over the bridge since he'd been waiting there. This was obviously not a busy part of town.

Drawing his cloak tightly around him, pushing his hat well down over his eyes, Ned crept out of his hiding place. He climbed onto the bridge and looked around. Nothing. He walked casually over to the corner, reaching the house without incident.

The ground-floor window was barred, of course, but it had a stone sill and a stone lintel. *I can climb up from the sill onto the lintel,* Ned thought. *I can reach the sill of that first-floor window—which is also shut—and from there leap sideways to the balcony.*

He looked around. No one. Cautiously, he approached the window. He looked around. The coast was clear. He climbed onto the windowsill. Now or never. He reached up for the lintel. He could just about touch it. He leaped up, got ahold of the lintel, and managed to haul himself up. He did not dare to look behind him now. If someone caught him at it, he wouldn't be able to explain. He must just pray for the best.

Not giving himself time to think, he sprang for the sill of the second window and scrambled onto it. Then he reached over to the balcony. In an instant he was standing there.

It had all been quite easy. But he had no time to congratulate himself. There was a door leading onto the balcony, a wooden door. It was shut. He tried it. In vain. He stared at it, nonplussed. What now? He tried the door again. Still locked. He tried to see through the keyhole, but could make out nothing, for the key was in the way. He put his shoulder to the door. But it was solid, and he did not dare push too hard against it, in case he made a noise which would alert the people inside.

Well, this is a fine to-do, thought Ned. *Here I am on the balcony, but I'm no better off than before. In fact, I may be worse off. If someone opens that door and comes out here, my goose will be well and truly cooked. Maybe I should just climb down again and wait under the bridge like before. I should not have been so impatient. But if I'd waited till nightfall, it would have been no different, would it? This door would still have been locked and I'd still be here all alone, unable to—*

Suddenly, he heard voices. They were from inside the house—from inside the room beyond the balcony! Panicking, he pressed himself against the wall to the side of the door, hoping against hope that if they opened the door they might not see him behind it. Now he could hear footsteps—and the voices grew louder. One of them, at least. It was a man's voice, and Ned thought he recognized the harsh tones of the scarred man, the supposed captain. The other was a woman's voice, a mere murmur. His hands sweated, his blood ran cold. It must be the Countess . . . and he was caught like a rat in a trap.

Please, God, please, don't let them open this door. Don't let them come out here. Don't let them see me.... He held his breath, fervently praying and wishing.

The door did not open. They didn't come out. He could hear them moving around, just beyond the door. They were still talking, low, fast, in Italian. He couldn't understand what they were saying. Then he heard a door slam, footsteps moving away. They must have gone out of the room.

Thank God, thank God.... He took a deep breath, swallowing the fear that had risen in his throat. He tiptoed to the railing and looked down into the street. Still no one. He had to get back down there. It was too dangerous to stay. And at that very moment, the balcony door rattled, creaked, and opened. And Ned, frozen in the act of throwing a leg over the railing, stared at the person who was standing in the doorway, looking as startled as he was.

It was not the Countess, and not the scarred man, and not Master Ashby, but a complete stranger: a girl of about his age or a little younger. A very lovely girl, slim, willowy, with creamy skin, and hair of a rich red-brown, and large, long-lashed dark eyes. She was dressed in a simple pale-brown dress with white trimmings that perfectly set off her beauty.

She stared at him. He stared back at her. He found his voice, first. '*Scusi*... I... not... I mean...' He trailed off. His mind had gone quite blank. He'd made a stupid mistake. He'd come to the wrong house. But he was sure this was the one the scarred man had gone into.

The girl's eyes widened. She said slowly, 'You . . . you not from Venice.' Her English was halting but understandable.

'No,' said Ned blankly. 'I'm English.' He thought she reminded him, very vaguely, of someone. Yes, the hair. The Count had hair of that sort of colour. Then he remembered hearing Dr Leone saying that the Montemoros had a daughter. A girl who didn't live with them. What was her name? He couldn't remember. This must be her. But what on earth was she doing here?

He said quickly, 'Please forgive me, your grace'—er, how did one address a Count's daughter?—'I was just . . . just looking for a friend of mine.' As he spoke, he was looking around the room. It was a small, neat, plain bedroom, with a made bed, a chair, and a table. No sign of Master Ashby.

'A friend?' said the girl, frowning.

'My friend,' said Ned, taking a little heart from the fact the girl hadn't screamed, or called for help. 'My master. His name is Mateo Ashby. Is he here?'

She stared at him. She repeated, 'You want Signor Ashby?' She pronounced the name with a charming Italian accent.

'Yes. Please—he's here, isn't he? Please help me. There's been some mistake, you see, and—'

Just then, the door at the other end of the room opened and the scarred man came in. He saw Ned at once. With an oath, he sprang across the room at him. He shouted unintelligibly in Ned's face, his eyes blazing with fury.

The girl ran to him and touched his arm. She said something fast to him. The scarred man turned his head to her. He made an explosive sound. Then, to Ned's astonished relief, he released him. But he stood glaring at him, his black eyes full of suspicion.

'Thank you,' said Ned to the girl. She shook her head.

'What your name?' she said carefully.

'Ned. Ned Fletcher.' Ned didn't think anything could be gained from lying now. But he kept a close eye on the scarred man. 'And Signor Ashby, he's my master. My boss. What's the word? Oh, yes. *Padrone. Mi padrone.*'

The girl's face cleared. 'Ah. Yes. You from Londra too.'

'Londra? Oh, yes, London. Master Ashby, me, his daughter Celia, his sister Mistress Quickly. We are from London. We—'

The scarred man interjected something then, and the girl answered sharply back. All Ned could understand was, 'No, Claudio.' But the scarred man subsided.

Ned said, 'Look, I think your guard—er, Claudio—is making a mistake. He should release my master—my *padrone.*' She looked at him, uncomprehending. He tried again. 'The Countess . . . your mother—er, your *mamma*—she has it wrong.' Pray God he was right, he thought, and these weren't actually a gang of ruthless pirates, because what would they make of what he was saying? But he was sure now it wasn't pirates they had to deal with.

She shook her head. 'My *mamma*? I not understand. I take you . . . to . . . the signor. You see him. You talk.'

'Why, thank you,' said Ned, mighty relieved. 'Thank you. You are most kind.'

She spoke briefly to Claudio. The man gave a hard look at Ned but did not argue. Clearly, he would do what the girl asked. But he kept close at Ned's heels as the latter followed the girl out of the room, along the hall, and down some stairs.

They reached a large hall, unusually panelled in different-coloured woods. Then, to his amazement, the girl stopped in front of one of the panels and fumbled with it. It slid open. Beyond was a dim space. She went through and beckoned Ned to do the same.

And there was Matthew Ashby. He was sitting reading on a narrow bed, in a room that smelled a little damp but was otherwise not unpleasant. There was a small window that gave onto the canal, a lamp on a table, a bright coverlet over the bed, and a small rug on the floor.

'Master Ashby!' cried Ned. 'Are you all right? Have they done anything to you?'

Ashby started up from the bed. 'Why, Ned! Whatever are you doing here! However did you get here?' He turned to Claudio and said something sharp in Italian. The man shrugged.

Ned watched this little scene in some astonishment. He said, 'Sir, what's going on? I don't understand. . . .'

'Where have you come from? Who's with you?' Master Ashby's voice was sharp, sharper than Ned had ever heard it.

He faltered, 'No one. I . . . I came from Venice. Dr Leone wanted to send me to the mainland. He let Henri stay with him, and—'

'Henri? What are you talking about?'

'Henri d'Arcy.' Swiftly, Ned explained.

Matthew Ashby exclaimed, 'A duel! Of all the stupid—'

'Well, sir,' snapped Ned, with some spirit, 'if we hadn't been there, we wouldn't have seen what happened to you.'

'That's just it,' said his master. 'It would have been better if you hadn't.' As Ned goggled at him, he went on, 'You see, it's not quite what you think. Now, tell me, Ned, were you followed?'

'No. I told you, Dr Leone thought I was going to the mainland. And I'm sure no one followed me.'

'Why did you choose Murano, then?'

'I just thought that I would do what I'd sworn to do—leave Venice—but also double back. I thought that way Dr Leone wouldn't know. There was no way I was going to be kept out of this investigation.'

'I see,' said Master Ashby. He turned to the silent girl and Claudio, and said something to them. They nodded. But Claudio's eyes had not lost their hard glare. He snapped a question.

'He asks how you tracked him down,' said the merchant.

'I didn't—it was sheer luck.' Ned explained what had happened and Master Ashby translated.

'Sir,' broke in Ned, 'please, you must explain to me what is going on. You're a prisoner here, yet you seem on good terms with these people. Why?'

'Because I'm not a prisoner, Ned,' said Matthew Ashby calmly. 'Not now. At first I was, till they realized who I am and why I was asking questions about Sarah.'

Ned felt completely at sea. 'I—I don't understand,' he faltered. 'Why would the Countess have you kidnapped and then—'

'The Countess?' Master Ashby stared at him. 'What do you mean?'

'Why, because that man works for her and that girl's her daughter, I suppose,' said Ned rather sarcastically.

Matthew Ashby stared. Then he burst out laughing. 'My poor Ned! You can put your mind at rest straight away. Claudio most certainly does not work for the Countess. His loyalties are quite elsewhere. I'm not sure by what tortuous route you came to the conclusion that this lovely girl could be that scheming Montemoro woman's daughter, but let me set your mind at rest.' He jumped up and took the girl's hand. 'Allow me to introduce you, Ned, to a most spirited and brave young woman, the person we have come so far to find—only to discover that she found us first. Yes, Ned, this is none other than Signorina Sarah Tedeschi!'

Mistress Quickly gets mad

Mistress Quickly was shouting. 'Anything could have happened to you! I thought someone had kidnapped you! I looked up and down these streets and couldn't see you! I was going to start a search party. . . .'

'I'm sorry to have worried you. But as you can see, I'm alive and well,' said Celia hurriedly. 'I'm sorry to have left you for so long, but I just went exploring a little and—'

'Stuff and nonsense!' said her aunt roundly. 'Tell fibs like that to your father if you like. He's an innocent soul. But I know what you've been up to. Snooping, eh? Chasing little hares of your own.'

Celia looked at her and decided that denial wasn't worth the trouble. 'Yes,' she said. 'I'm afraid so, Aunt Bess. I went to call on Dr Tedeschi.'

'Oh, I knew it was too good to be true that you'd let the men take care of things! Do you mean to say you've been in the Ghetto by yourself?'

'It was perfectly safe. And I learned some very interesting things. Aunt Bess, please listen. We've got to get back to Dr Leone's house straight away. Then I have to find Ned and bring him back to Dr Tedeschi's with me. Something's happened, something very important. Can you tell Father where we are and tell him to meet us there as soon as possible?'

'Why don't you tell him yourself?'

'This is around his nap-time, isn't it? And I can't wait. Besides, he always asks so many anxious questions. And you're so good at managing him, Aunt Bess.'

'I'm not surprised he's anxious, you're such a trial,' grumbled Mistress Quickly, but her colour was subsiding and she didn't look quite as cross. 'Very well, get in the boat and let's be going. But I'm afraid, my dear, that you are going to have to tell me everything before we get to the house. If I am to persuade my brother into more tomfoolery, I am not going to be kept in ignorance by a chit of a girl.' She settled herself down on the cushions and fixed Celia with a gimlet eye. 'Begin.'

It took nearly the entire way back for Celia to tell Mistress Quickly the whole story, including what had happened in Cannaregio and the Ghetto the day before. When Celia finished, she waited cautiously to see how Mistress Quickly would react.

She was silent for quite a few minutes, then said, 'You take my breath away, Celia Margaret Ashby.'

Oh dear, thought Celia, *she only calls me by my full name if she's really annoyed with me.*

'You really do,' went on Mistress Quickly. 'Do you realize just how madly you have behaved? You put yourself into appalling danger—and for what? So you can prove to Ned that you can do as well as he? What kind of ridiculous notion is this? This isn't a game, Celia. This is about people's lives. That Sarah, she removed herself from her father because she was afraid for him; she didn't want to put him in danger while she did her little investigation. But you've just thought of yourself. You haven't thought of us at all—you haven't even imagined what it might be like for us if something happens to you!' Her eyes glittered. 'Have you?'

Celia faltered, 'You . . . you don't understand. I didn't think that—'

'No, you *didn't* think, did you? You just acted. You just did whatever you thought was best. You didn't ask if it was best for others. Now that poor doctor and his sister are stuck with some trussed-up villain and they're no closer to their Sarah!'

'It wasn't my fault Marco came to Tartuffo—' began Celia, annoyed, but her aunt cut her off.

'No, it wasn't your fault, but you didn't improve matters, did you, with your babbling to him the day before!'

'But how was I to know he was an informer? Besides, I *did* improve matters!' snapped Celia, incensed. 'Tartuffo was sent off with his tail between his legs and Marco can't go running off to the Countess. And I know who the madman is, so they can talk to him and find out where his friend is! I'm sure he's the one who's hiding Sarah!'

'Pish, you know nothing of the kind. Why do you believe the lies of that Marco?'

'It's not him, Aunt Bess! It's the Tedeschis. They think he could be the key to Sarah's disappearance.'

'What use will a madman be, anyway?' said her aunt, changing tack. 'By their very nature, madmen can't answer sensible questions.'

'He may not always be mad,' said Celia hopefully. 'Dr Tedeschi said it was the kind of madness that comes and goes with the moon.'

'Doctors!' said Mistress Quickly with great scorn.

'Well, here we are, Aunt Bess. Will you help me, or just read me lectures on my folly?'

'Tush, the cheek of the child! You really are the limit, Celia Margaret Ashby,' said her aunt crossly. 'But I suppose now you have put us all on the line and there is no help for it but to continue as best we can. Yes, I will help you, but you must—'

'Aunt Bess, you are the dearest person alive!' said Celia, throwing her arms around Mistress Quickly's neck and kissing her on the cheek. 'I really am sorry for worrying you, and I'm sorry I was selfish—I didn't mean to be—and I think you're right, I was being too proud . . . but you do understand, this is important and I *must* do it.'

'Hmm,' said Mistress Quickly, pink again, but with pleasure this time. 'Promise me, though, that you will be more careful in future.'

'I promise!' said Celia gaily. She sprang out of the boat and onto the landing-stage and ran up the steps towards Dr Leone's house, calling, 'Ned, Ned, where are you?'

'Child, child, a little more decorum,' Mistress Quickly called after her as she puffed and panted in an effort to keep up.

'What do you mean, Ned's gone?' Celia had come into the hall to find Dr Leone hurrying down the stairs towards her, his mane of hair askew, his usually confident manner a little uncertain.

Now he turned to Mistress Quickly. 'I'm sorry, signora, but there's trouble. Real trouble. You and the young lady must follow Ned at once and get to safety.'

'Follow Ned where?' said Celia, bewildered, while at the same time Mistress Quickly snapped, 'And I'll trouble you not to order Celia and me around, Dr Leone. Where is my brother? I want to speak to him at once.'

'I'm afraid that's not possible,' said Dr Leone. 'You see, he—'

'What do you mean, "not possible"? Nonsense! Is he in his room? I shall go and see him at once.'

Mistress Quickly picked up her skirts and made for the stairs.

'I mean, he's gone too,' said Dr Leone helplessly.

Mistress Quickly stopped. 'What do you mean, "gone too"?'

'He . . .' Dr Leone swallowed. 'I'm afraid your brother has been kidnapped, signora.'

Mistress Quickly went chalk-white. 'Whatever do you mean?'

'Last night he was lured into an assignation with someone, but it was a trap. He was abducted.'

'What! Why didn't you tell us?' cried Mistress Quickly. 'Last night, you say! But that's hours ago! How long have you known!'

'Since . . . since . . . er . . . last night. We . . . we are trying to find him.'

'We? Is that where Ned's gone, Dr Leone?' said Celia. 'To find him?'

'No . . . no . . . He . . . Well, he wanted to tell you and Mistress Quickly last night about what happened to Mateo, but I . . . I persuaded him it wasn't a good idea. I've sent him to the mainland, to my house in Arqua. I thought he'd be safe there. . . . You see,' said Dr Leone in a rather small voice, as the eyes of the two women fixed on him, 'he *saw* Mateo being abducted. . . . I mean, he saw the kidnappers, and so I thought he'd be . . . Well, he and Henri were both there, but Henri rather later, so I don't think he's in as much danger, and—'

'But why were they there?' said Celia blankly.

Dr Leone looked at her and gave a faint smile. 'I believe they'd arranged a duel. By coincidence, it was at the same spot where Mateo went. Henri was late for it, which was why he didn't see as much as Ned did.'

'A duel?'

Dr Leone's smile grew broader. 'I believe—well, Henri as much as implied to me—it was over *you,* signorina.'

'Me?' Colour rushed scarlet into Celia's cheeks. 'But . . .' She swallowed. 'But if they'd fought, Ned could have been hurt, or even killed!'

'He could, yes,' said Dr Leone. After a short pause, he added, watching Celia carefully, 'As could Henri, of course.'

'I'm sure Henri can much better look after himself,' said Celia lightly. 'But Ned . . . Ned rushes into things. He would swing wildly. . . .' She blushed again. Her eyes sparkled angrily. 'Oh, I'm going to box his ears when I see him! I'm going to really let him know what I think, and—'

'He is a brave young man, signorina,' broke in Dr Leone gently. 'He tried to fight off Mateo's attackers and was knocked out for his pains.'

From red, Celia went pale. 'Is he . . . is he all right?'

'Oh, yes, he's fine. He has a hard head, this young man of yours.'

She didn't say crossly, 'He's not *mine*.' She merely said, 'Did he want to be sent away?'

Dr Leone smiled. 'No. He was very angry about it. He most certainly did not want to go.'

'I'm not surprised,' said Celia warmly, 'being packed off like unwanted luggage.'

Mistress Quickly said tartly, 'And if you think *I'm* going to be packed off as easily as Ned, Dr Leone, you are in for a surprise. I am not leaving here while my brother is missing.'

'But, signora—'

'No "but"s, sir. I am not moving. Or at least only to give whoever's responsible for this outrage a good piece of my mind. I suppose it is that Countess person?'

'We think so . . . ,' said Dr Leone hesitantly. 'Henri has gone to get his father's help; I said that I would wait here for you and make sure you left safely.'

'We're not going,' said Mistress Quickly. 'At least, I'm not. My niece will want to go after her—after Ned, perhaps, and bring him back. We need his help, Dr Leone.'

'But I told you, it's not safe for him here, now that the Countess has clapped eyes on him, and— Oh, sorry, I must tell you that too, I suppose.' And he told them what had happened at Ca' Montemoro.

Celia and her aunt looked at each other. 'We saw you,' said Bess Quickly.

Dr Leone stared. 'What?'

'On the canal,' said Celia. 'I just knew Ned and the rest of you had gone off investigating on your own!'

'He didn't want to go without you,' said Dr Leone gently. 'It was I who told him he must not involve you.'

'Of all the cheek!' said Celia crossly, but with a little glow in her heart all the same. So Ned had not tried to trick her, or leave her out of things. . . . 'There is more, Dr Leone,' she said, and filled him in on what had happened at the Tedeschis'.

Dr Leone gave a gusty sigh. 'Dear God, this is a tangled web and no mistake.'

'Ned described the man in the alley, the supposed captain, as having the bearing of a soldier?' said Celia.

'Yes. Exactly. Either we have two lots of soldiers—some working for the Countess, some helping Sarah—or we have one. And in that case, either they're working for the Countess, *or* for Sarah.'

'If it's Sarah's friend, perhaps he only took Father because he was afraid he was asking too many questions and didn't know why,' said Celia excitedly.

'Perhaps. That would be the best alternative, of course. But if he is working for the Countess—then he's holding Sarah, as well as Mateo. And that means . . .'

'It means,' said Celia, 'that he's been holding Sarah

for weeks. Why hasn't the Countess done anything to her, in all that time?'

'Perhaps she has,' said Dr Leone grimly.

'No, he can't, because why then take Father too? It doesn't make sense. If it's the Countess who has arranged this, then she has simply been keeping Sarah out of circulation for some time. And there has to be a reason for that. We have to find that man and speak to him.'

'He'll have gone to ground,' said Dr Leone. 'Where do we start looking?'

'We have to find his friend. The madman,' said Celia. 'I wish . . . I wish Ned were here. He saw him first. He spoke to him. I only saw him passing by.' She looked at the other two. 'I will go and look for the madman. Will you please go back to Dr Tedeschi and tell him what has happened? He and his sister have a right to know everything.'

'Of course,' said Dr Leone, 'but, my dear young lady, it is not safe for you to go hunting madmen in the streets by yourself, and—'

'Pish!' said Celia fiercely. 'I'm not afraid! I'm going, and that's that.'

'Really, I must protest. Signora,' began Dr Leone, turning to Mistress Quickly for support. 'Surely you cannot allow—'

'My niece is a determined and brave young woman,' said Mistress Quickly tartly. 'I should be wasting my breath if I attempted to dissuade her. She will be careful, she has promised me that, and I do not think she will break that promise. Her heart is set on helping her father and her young man. And frankly, I share her wish. No, don't open your mouth and protest, Dr Leone. It is decided, and that is that.'

'I had heard Englishwomen were headstrong,' grumbled Dr Leone, 'but this is really beyond—'

'We have a queen with a heart of oak and sinews of steel,' said Mistress Quickly proudly, 'so it is perhaps not so surprising we do not consider ourselves weak and feeble creatures.'

'Power is not generally good for a woman,' said Dr Leone sententiously. 'Think of that Countess. Now, there's an example of how power goes to the head of a woman.'

Mistress Quickly folded her arms and looked at him. 'Women are *people,* Dr Leone. We're not all good, all bad, or all indifferent. It takes all kinds to make any world. Now then, if you have stopped lecturing us on our own sex, Dr Leone, have you made up your mind: are you coming with me to the Ghetto, or must I go there on my own?'

'My dear signora!' he said in a scandalized tone. 'I most certainly will accompany you. The very idea of your going alone! Besides, I have met the good doctor and know where he lives.'

'I am sure I would find it, if Celia gave me directions,' said Mistress Quickly primly. 'But you may come with me if you wish.' On her way to the door, sailing out like a stately galleon with Dr Leone as a lesser craft behind her, she stopped, turned, and said to Celia, 'Good luck, my dear. And take great care. We must meet back here in an hour to report on what we have found.'

'Yes, Aunt Bess,' said Celia meekly, but with a big smile on her face. Clearly, Mistress Quickly had the bit between her teeth now and nothing was going to stop her! *Or me, either,* she thought defiantly. *Me or Ned. Dear Ned* . . . She could just imagine how angry he'd have been at being sent out of the action. And anger made him stubborn. She'd seen it often enough. So would he really have meekly done as the bossy Venetian alchemist wanted?

GAMBLERS

'This is how it happened,' said Master Ashby comfortably. 'Captain Battaglia—that's Claudio, here—sent a secret message to me at Orlando's house. He'd heard I'd been to Dr Tedeschi's house and was afraid I was working for the Countess. So he had me seized.'

Ned shook himself from his astonishment. 'I know that, sir. Remember, I was there. Anyway, I saw Claudio, and—'

Here Claudio interrupted. He was smiling faintly.

'He said you're not a bad fighter and he's sorry if his

friends hurt you,' said Ashby, raising an eyebrow. 'I must say you look all right, Ned.'

'I am perfectly all right,' said Ned, grinning. 'Though there's a good bruise under all this hair, somewhere. Still, no hard feelings.' He held out a hand to Claudio. The other took it and shook. Now his smile was broad. It quite transformed his hard face, so that he looked both a good deal younger and a good deal more handsome.

Sarah said anxiously, 'Friends now, yes?'

'Yes,' said Ned. He looked at her. How lovely she was! As lovely as a painting. He caught Claudio's glance and knew at once that the young soldier was in love with her. But did she love him? Impossible to tell. He felt a sudden surge of fellow-feeling for him. 'I don't understand. Why is Claudio hiding you? I mean, how did you know him? What is this place?'

She smiled. 'This house—Claudio *padre*.'

'It belongs to Claudio's father? Where is he?'

'His father's dead,' interrupted Master Ashby. 'Claudio's the only child. So the house is his now.'

'Why did they have a secret room?'

'Oh, lots of houses hereabouts have them. Bolt-holes, you know, if things get sticky.'

'But how did Sarah meet him?'

'She told me he owed her father a good deal—Dr Tedeschi treated his sick friend, whom no other doctor wanted to touch. Claudio is a man of great loyalty. Sarah asked him to help her, so he did.'

'But . . . what have they been doing all this time?'

Sarah flushed. Obviously she had understood. She said, low, hard, 'Claudio help me.'

'They've been trying to gather evidence against the Countess,' said the merchant. 'Evidence that will show she's been targeting Sarah because she thinks she knows something.'

'Knows what?'

'That the Countess is guilty of a crime. A serious, even massive crime. She wants to silence Sarah but dares not move against her openly.'

'Did they find anything out?'

'A rather ugly story to do with a crooked trader from Verona, called Gamboretto.'

'What!' said Ned, astonished. 'But that's . . .'

Master Ashby nodded grimly. 'Exactly. The very same Gamboretto whose name Salerio's son mentioned. Now, Sarah has uncovered some evidence that the Montemoros may be involved with this crook Gamboretto and his friends, the pirates.'

'Involved in *piracy*? But they're rich. Dr Leone said rich as Midas. So why—'

'Greed, my boy. Greed and most likely a love of danger.'

'But still!' Ned was aghast. 'These pirates don't only steal cargoes and bankrupt merchants; they've murdered countless innocent men. How could a family like that be involved in such wicked, wicked things?'

Ashby sighed. 'My dear boy, you are very young. The wickedness of the world knows no bounds. Besides, the Montemoros must feel they're above suspicion. They've got away with it for years, if they truly are involved. And you must understand, that is by no means certain. But there are suggestive links—'

'God's blood!' burst out Ned. 'And we raced right into the wolf's den with our stories about pirates kidnapping you!' Seeing the others' bewilderment he quickly recounted to them what had happened at the Montemoro house. 'She didn't betray herself at all,' he finished. 'If she's involved with these pirates, then she's being very cool about it all.'

'I don't think she's the sort of woman who is easily frightened,' said Master Ashby. 'She's a high-stakes gambler, with an ice-cold hand. And heart. But Claudio has heard rumours that the Duke's secret police may also be investigating Gamboretto and his links in Venice. If that's so, then what I have to tell them of our own losses may also help to build a case. And confirmation of those links could be disastrous for the Montemoros.'

'But what are those links?'

'Circumstantial evidence, really. Nothing rock-solid as yet. The Montemoros travel to Verona on occasion, for they have a villa in the countryside—which is where their daughter Isabella lives, by the way, with her da Piero uncle's family. They may have a connection with Gamboretto—a member of their household has been seen at the man's house on at least one occasion. Add to that the fact they have extensive interests in shipping and that, though their ships ply the same shipping lanes as those haunted by the pirates, they have never lost a single ship, crewman, or piece of cargo. Mind you, that's the case for other Venetian families, so that can't really be held against them. But after pirate attacks have bankrupted other merchants, Gamboretto offers to buy up their remaining stock. There is evidence that some of that has ended up in Montemoro hands. And there's a hint—though it's not yet proven—that at least one of the pirates may once have been in the employ of Maffei, the head of the Montemoro guards. There's a good deal more of the same sort. Nothing definite. But suggestive. Dangerously so.'

Ned's head whirled. 'But why would the Countess think Sarah knew anything about all this? She didn't, did she, before?'

Ashby shook his head. 'No. It's only since then that Sarah has been ferreting around. But the Countess may fear the very worst: she may think the Count *told* Sarah about it on that fateful day.'

Ned stared. 'But that's absurd! Why on earth would he?'

'You said yourself he looked jumpy. Haunted. Frightened. Maybe his conscience is troubling him.'

'But if they are involved with piracy and murder on

the high seas, it's probably been going on for years, as you said. Why on earth should he get scared now?'

'Maybe he's heard the secret police are after him. Or maybe . . . who knows what goes on in men's souls? Maybe he feels remorse about all those many deaths, all those poor sailors slaughtered on the high seas. Stranger things have happened.' Ashby turned to the girl. 'Sarah, tell him what the Count said to you.'

Sarah's eyes were very bright. 'He ask if sick woman soon well. I say I hope so. He ask if I . . . if Papa—he my *padre,* yes, or my . . . my *marito*?'

'If Dr Tedeschi was her father or her husband,' explained Master Ashby.

Ned raised his eyebrows.

'It's not what you think,' said Ashby. 'Tell him, Sarah.'

'I say he my *padre,*' went on Sarah. 'He say, ah. Then he ask where my *mamma*. I say she *morte*.'

'Dead,' said Ashby. 'And then he asked one more question. And that's when the guard came in. He must have overheard him. She never had time to reply. You understand, his wife has him watched by her guards. It appears, though, that he momentarily managed to give them the slip when he came into the sickroom.'

'But what was that last question?'

'Do I know Verona,' said Sarah.

'What?'

'He asked if she knew Verona,' said Master Ashby.

'You know, the city of Verona. It meant nothing to her then—she thought it was just idle small talk. He seemed preoccupied, you see, staring out of the window. She had no idea then about Gamboretto from Verona, of course, and the way that man's been linked to the pirates. But now she wonders if the Count was indeed about to confide in her.'

'But why?'

'Look at her,' said Ashby simply. 'He came into that sickroom and saw her tending to his sick relative. Maybe she seemed like an angel of mercy to him. Who knows? Or maybe he just needed to unburden himself to someone. It seems that the man's weak, unreliable at the best of times. And perhaps he is feeling the pressure too greatly now, if the Duke's secret police really are on their track.' He turned to Claudio and Sarah. 'I think it is time.'

'Time for what?' said Ned, but there was no answer, for the other three were talking in Italian amongst themselves. Ned said, 'What's going on? You must tell me.'

'It's this,' said Ashby. 'In light of everything, we've just decided to bring our plan forward.'

'Plan? What plan?'

'My dear boy, as the Countess now has a description of Claudio—and will connect him with my disappearance, and thence perhaps to Sarah—it's best we surprise her before she surprises us.'

'What do you mean?' said Ned, very uneasy.

Sarah said, 'We see Contessa. We tell her, *now*.'

Ned stared at her. 'Tell her what? That you think she's a crook, hand in glove with murderous pirates? Are you crazy? She'll have you arrested in two seconds. Or killed, more likely.'

'No, no, you not know, you . . .' Frustrated, the girl turned to the merchant and rattled away in Italian.

Master Ashby turned to Ned. 'She says it's enough, she's had enough of hiding. She is sure the Countess is guilty. The time has come to confront her. She was planning to do this later, but now events have forced her hand. She's going to make the Countess confess.'

Ned was aghast. 'How? Does she plan to blackmail her? Master Ashby, please tell Sarah she's mad.'

He shook his head, smiling a little. 'I don't think she is, Ned. Not at all. Indeed, I think this plan of hers has merit.'

'What! The Countess will make mincemeat of her. And if she doesn't have a witness—someone who can prove that the Countess is in this up to her neck—then she doesn't stand a chance.'

'She does have a witness.'

'Who?'

'The Count.'

Ned stared at Sarah. '*The Count?* But he's much too scared to help you. And Dr Leone thinks he's going to be locked up now, prevented from talking to anybody. It's madness!' He turned to Claudio. 'Please, you must make her understand. . . . She cannot do this, alone or with you. The Countess will just kill you both!'

Claudio looked at him and shrugged. Ashby said, 'Ned, you don't understand. They don't propose to go there alone, but with some of his soldier friends from the other night—and me.'

'But how will you get in?'

'Claudio has watched the Montemoro palace many times. He says the guards are rather lazy. The palace hasn't been attacked for many years, so they take things for granted.'

'It's true they didn't challenge us till we were almost on them,' said Ned, remembering.

'And it's especially so at nightfall, when we plan to go. The guards play cards. And there are many back entrances where the men and I can slip in. Sarah will be officially announced, though. I am sure the Countess will receive her.'

'I'm sure the Countess will be delighted to do so,' cried Ned. 'Come into my web, said the spider to the fly. No, it can't be done. Even with the others, it's madness. Self-slaughter.'

'No. Not if the Duke knows about it too,' said his master firmly. 'That's the other part of the plan. You are to go back to Orlando's house, tell him what's happened, and together you go and see the Duke. He must be told everything and persuaded to take action at once.'

'But how can you be sure that he will act?'

'If his secret police already suspect a link between Gamboretto and the Montemoros, then the Countess's confession will confirm it, beyond doubt.'

'But what if nothing happens—I mean, if neither the Count nor the Countess says anything incriminating? Then the Duke's men will just hear a hysterical girl—a hysterical *Jewish* girl—meddling in a very murky affair indeed. Accusing a prominent family without proof. And then where will she be? Sarah thinks the Count will be a witness against his wife. She must be mad. He'd have everything to lose if he told the truth. It is a crazy gamble.'

'Then why did he mention Verona to Sarah, eh?' said Ashby triumphantly. 'And why did he ask *you,* a complete stranger, if you'd take on a commission for him? He must be feeling either guilty, or frightened, or both. The man's cracking and there's no telling at all what he might do.'

'Exactly,' said Ned, 'that's why I—'

'Look, Ned, it's no use arguing.' Ashby's face was flushed, his eyes shining.

'Oh, sir! I can't believe you think it's a good idea,' said Ned despairingly.

'But I do. You see, Ned, things have gone on for long enough. This woman must be stopped. We have right on our side. God has protected Sarah and Claudio all this time—and I think He will continue to do so.'

'But we have to give Him a helping hand sometimes,' protested Ned.

'Exactly.' Matthew Ashby beamed. 'I knew you'd understand. That's just what we are doing. Helping ourselves as well. The time is past for discretion and secrecy. We have to take the fight to the enemy's camp!'

'But Sarah's father . . .'

'Sarah thinks he will understand and support her.'

'Oh, dear,' said Ned.

'Are you going to help or not?'

'Of course I am,' sighed Ned, 'but I wish that—'

'Then it's settled.' Matthew Ashby turned to Sarah and told her.

She smiled. It was a dazzling smile that lit up her whole face and made her seem even more beautiful. 'Thank you,' she murmured, looking into his eyes. 'My heart say thank you, thank you.'

'Not—not at all,' he faltered, scarlet to the tips of his ears and aware that Claudio was watching him. 'It . . . I mean . . . anyone would . . . er . . .'

'Stop talking, Ned, and get going,' said Master Ashby briskly. 'Get back to Orlando's as quickly as you can and tell him to go at once to the Duke and organize things.'

'Yes, sir,' said Ned, and fled.

The Madman of Venice

Celia walked along briskly, looking in every doorway, every alley, every spot where a madman might take shelter. Ned had first seen him on the way to Dr Leone's, and then they'd both seen him in Cannaregio, so she had decided to retrace their footsteps back to St Mark's Square first and then go to Cannaregio by boat. She came to the little square Ned had described. Yes. There was the church. But there was no one in the doorway.

She was about to move on when she heard music. It

came from inside the church. On an impulse she pushed open the heavy door and peered in.

The church was dim, fragrant with incense and crowded with worshipers. A young man was singing, accompanied by three or four instruments. It was soaringly beautiful music—heavenly music, she thought. And the singer's high voice was almost inhuman—no, sexless. Angelic. A strange delight filled her; her soul was stirred. She seemed to see another world opening before her; something trembling on the edge of consciousness, just beyond.

And then, quite suddenly, she saw *him*—a twisted wreck of a man with tangled white hair, not huddling fearfully, or shambling aimlessly, but on his knees in a pew at the very back, his head in his hands. No one was near him; they all kept their distance from him, for he smelled bad. Yet no one told him to go. This was the house of God, from which even sad dregs of humanity like this one could not be barred.

Celia slipped into the church and into the pew where he knelt. He did not look up at her. He seemed to be praying. But his shoulders were heaving, and she thought he was weeping as well. She did not want to intrude into either his grief or his prayers, but she was determined not to let him go before she'd had a chance to speak to him. She dropped her own head to her hands, taking care that she could see sideways between her fingers. She cringed as a whiff of his odour reached her.

Oh, God, he did smell dreadful. And he looked worse. She tried to control the revulsion that rose up in her throat. *Stop it,* she told herself. *You have been blessed. Fortunate. Unlike this poor lost soul.* Yet safe in her own good fortune, she had no care for his misery, his degradation; no, she had come here just to use him for her investigation. To pester him with questions, so she could prove herself. Suddenly, she felt ashamed. A vista of sadness opened before her, a sudden glimpse into someone else's suffering. Someone else's story . . .

The music reached a crescendo. The singer's unearthly voice rose above it like a skylark in the clear air. All at once Celia found that she was crying too. The tears ran down her fingers and she couldn't stop them.

Suddenly, she felt a light touch on her shoulder. A timid finger, quickly withdrawn. She turned her head to one side and saw the madman looking at her out of deep-set, gentle blue eyes. So gentle was his gaze that for a moment she thought she must be mistaken. This wasn't the raving lunatic Ned had talked about, the crazy man Dr Tedeschi had treated. This was some other man.

And then he spoke. Softly, wonderingly. Just one word. But it made Celia start. 'Beatrice,' he said, and in the whisper was all the longing of the world. 'Beatrice,' he repeated. He reached out a hand again and touched her lightly on the shoulder, as if assuring himself she was real. 'Beatrice,' he said once more, and his face was suddenly suffused with an unearthly joy.

'I'm not . . . ,' began Celia, and then checked herself as an unexpected insight came to her. His mind was full of phantoms. And to him she must look like the phantom he most longed for, his lost Beatrice. She knew instinctively it was best not to dissuade him. So she reached out and touched his hand gently. She whispered, 'Come outside. Come with me.'

She swished out of the pew and he followed meekly, like a lamb.

'You have changed. You speak good English now,' he murmured when they were outside. 'Oh, Beatrice! I thought I would never find you again.'

His voice was calm, almost too calm. And how thin he was, how gaunt, how suffering had etched its harsh way into his features! With a surge of hot pity, Celia wondered what his story was. He was English, that was clear; but from what he'd said, his Beatrice was not. What had happened to her? Had she married someone else and gone away, and was she a comfortable matron somewhere, with a brood of children? Or was she dead?

'You have been to England,' she tried.

He shook his head. 'In the Lower Countries, and in Sicily, and oh, everywhere in the sad, violent world. To forget.'

'You went as a soldier?'

'Yes. War is hell. Life was hell. But now . . .' He smiled. 'Now Heaven has opened and you are here.'

Her heart turned over. Oh, this was too cruel! She could not go on. But something made her say, 'Where is your home? Where are your friends?'

'Home? I have none. Only with you.'

'But you . . . you've stayed with friends? Here in Venice?'

He looked at her, his eyes devouring her face. 'Claudio wanted me to stay with him, but I would not. You see, I had to search the city for you.'

Her ears pricked up. 'Claudio? Was he the one who took you to the doctor?'

He stared at her. 'Doctor? Yes. Perhaps. I . . . I am confused. Claudio is a good friend.'

'I should like you to take me to him,' she said gently.

He looked at her, the shadows gathering in his eyes. 'Why, Beatrice?'

'I should like to thank him for . . . for looking after you,' she said through the lump in her throat.

'Not now. Not now. Not now.' There was a rising note of panic in his voice. Celia saw the danger at once and made a rapid decision.

'I will take you home with me,' she said gently. 'Will you come?' He nodded, his smile beatific.

Taking his hand, she led him unresisting back through the streets to Dr Leone's house. She hoped desperately that the others might be back at the house by now. She did not think she could bear this piteous predicament for very much longer. Nothing had ever prepared her for this, and for the first time in her life, she felt uncertain, rudderless and utterly confused. *If only Ned were here . . .*

He wasn't there, of course. But at least Dr Leone and Mistress Quickly were, and Dr Tedeschi had come with them. To her great relief, the doctor grasped the situation right away. He led the madman gently from the room, murmuring soothing things to him all the while, playing the fiction that he was in 'Beatrice's' employ and would take care of the man's needs. It was extraordinary how gentle the doctor was and how the poor man seemed to trust him.

When they were alone, Celia said brokenly, 'It's just . . . just horrible. He thinks I'm his Beatrice. I let him think it. I feel like a fraud. A cruel fraud.'

'But he's the man we've been looking for?' said Dr Leone uncomfortably.

She nodded.

'You found out the name of his friend?'

She swallowed. 'Claudio. The friend's name is Claudio.'

Dr Leone shrugged. 'That's not much to go on—there must be dozens of Claudios in Venice.'

Mistress Quickly snorted indignantly. 'Celia has done excellent work.'

'It doesn't feel like excellent work,' Celia said sadly. 'It feels like I have coldly pirated a man's secret heart.'

Mistress Quickly looked at her, eyebrows raised. 'That doesn't sound like you, Celia.'

She shrugged. 'It's what I feel.'

'You did not tell him you *were* Beatrice,' pointed out Mistress Quickly, comfortingly. 'He took you for her, and in that joyful fancy he was happy for a while. It is a kindness you have done him, not a cruelty. And now he is safely in Dr Tedeschi's hands, which is the best possible place for him to be.'

'Yes. I suppose so.'

'And Dr Tedeschi will be able to get more out of him, I'll wager,' said Dr Leone briskly. 'Now stop fretting about it, Celia, and listen to this—when we went to Dr Tedeschi's, Marco was awake.'

'What did he say?'

'Mostly swearing at first, I'm afraid,' said Dr Leone. 'Such language! I quite blushed for Mistress Quickly's ears.'

'You could have spared your blushes, then,' Celia's aunt said tartly, 'for I don't understand much Italian, and besides, I'm sure I've heard worse than that in my time.'

'I made him understand that his tongue would have to loosen—and pretty smartly too,' said Dr Leone with a grim chuckle. 'A sword-point to the throat does wonders, you know. Anyway, he confirmed what we suspected—he's a small-time informer who's worked for the Montemoros at odd times. Not often; he's not considered too reliable. He didn't say he wasn't, of course, but I read between the lines of what he was saying.'

'Was it the Countess who sent him to the Ghetto?'

'It was Maffei, the head of the Countess's guards. Maffei has been with the Countess since before her marriage—he is fanatically loyal to her. He said Maffei told him about our visit—described Ned, asked if he'd seen anyone like that around the Ghetto—and Marco realized it was the young Englishman he'd spoken to the day before.' Dr Leone shook his head. 'I told you it was a dangerous thing to do! Anyway—he was sent to see if the Tedeschis reacted to this mention of Ned, or whether your beloved was employed by the Duke, or someone else. But being the vicious creature he is, Marco thought he'd increase his own pleasure by sullying Sarah's reputation as well. He knew about Tartuffo's feud with the Tedeschis, you see, and thought he could use it to his own advantage.'

'A dirty dog,' said Celia with feeling.

'Indeed. I'd dump him in the canal, still trussed up, if it were left up to me, but Jacob won't hear of it. He says we should just let him cool his heels for a while in the locked room, while we find this soldier—this Claudio.'

'He may know nothing about Sarah, of course,' said Celia rather glumly. 'He may have had nothing to do with her at all after he left their house with his mad friend.'

'Actually, he had a great deal to do with her, and what's more, with your father too,' said Ned, coming panting into the room at that very moment. He grinned to see their astonished faces. 'Didn't think you could get rid of me so easily, did you, Dr Leone? And I'm sorry, Celia, I really am, about not telling you at once about—'

'Hush,' she said, flying to his side. He took her hand and pressed it to his lips for a fleeting instant, then dropped it as she blushed scarlet. 'Oh, N-Ned,' she stammered, not looking at him, 'tell us, Ned, tell us quickly what you mean and what's happened!'

But before Ned could find his voice to answer, Dr Tedeschi returned. 'Our poor friend is settled now,' he said. 'His name is Edmund. I do not know his family name. He says he lived in Venice years ago, as a hired man-at-arms. But something happened to make him flee the city and take to war instead. This Claudio was someone he met then, on campaign. They have soldiered together.' He caught sight of Ned and raised an eyebrow.

'Dr Tedeschi, this is my Ned . . . I mean, my friend I told you about,' said Celia, blushing even more as the imprudent words came out of her mouth.

'Glad to meet you at last, Doctor,' said Ned happily. 'Very, very glad.' But his eyes were on Celia as he spoke. There was a little silence.

Dr Leone coughed. 'Why are you here, Ned? Why aren't you—'

Ned broke in. 'Dr Tedeschi, what I have to say concerns you more than anyone else in this room. At least, it is the closest to your heart.'

The doctor went very pale. So pale that it looked for an instant as though he was going to faint. 'My daughter . . . ,' he whispered. 'You have seen my daughter? She is . . . she is . . .'

'She is very well,' said Ned cheerfully. 'And sends her dearest love to you. This is how I met her. . . .'

The Quality of Mercy

It was a short time later and they were in the golden splendour of the Ducal Palace, in the presence of the Duke. He was a thin-faced old man with impassive dark eyes and a smartly trimmed white beard. Flanked by a couple of his men, he sat and listened quietly as Dr Leone told him the whole story. When the alchemist had finished, the Duke said nothing for a moment, appearing to be lost in thought. They waited anxiously.

At last the Duke spoke. He said, 'This is an extraordinary story, Orlando. Quite extraordinary.' His glance flicked over them and Celia's heart sank. He was not going to take them seriously. At best, he was just going to dismiss them. At worst . . .

'These are very serious allegations to make against one of our leading families, Orlando,' continued the Duke. 'You do understand that?'

'I do, your grace,' said Dr Leone, bowing low. 'And I would not have come to you if I were not utterly convinced indeed as to the seriousness of these allegations—which I believe are genuinely based on solid fact.'

The Duke sighed. 'Yes. I do see that. And I know your judgement in other matters to be sound.' He was silent a moment more; then he said, 'This is not entirely new to me. Our own investigations . . .' He broke off. 'It has not been easy to obtain information, and if this works, it will be a good thing. If there is one thing that can destroy Venice as much as Ottoman attacks from without, it is corruption from within. It is a cancer that spreads all too quickly. Very well, you shall have your men-at-arms.'

'Thank you, your grace,' said Dr Leone, beaming. 'I know well your reputation for great probity, and I knew you would hate the notion of the good name of Venice being besmirched in this manner by this wicked woman, who—'

'Wait,' said the Duke. He glanced at Dr Tedeschi, who was standing behind Dr Leone and hadn't spoken all this time. 'There is one thing: if the Countess does not confess, then the girl will be arrested.'

Fear leaped into the doctor's face. 'But, your grace . . .'

The Duke was expressionless. 'It will never do for a Jew to be seen to make an accusation against a Christian without proper proof. You people are protected under the law from those who would wish to harm you without cause, but if you seek to needlessly harm others or take revenge for imagined wrongs, then you will be punished.'

There was a little silence. Then the doctor spoke. His voice was low and shook a little, his face was pale. But his eyes didn't waver. 'Your grace,' he said, 'this is no *imagined* wrong, but a vicious attempt to destroy my daughter's good name and reputation, in order to hide an even greater sin. My daughter is an innocent caught up in the ugly machinations of those much more powerful than she. We want no revenge—but justice.'

'And you shall have it, if that is so,' said the Duke. His impassive face had not changed at all during the doctor's speech. 'But you must also understand there are consequences for all actions in this world.'

'I understand, your grace,' said Dr Tedeschi very quietly. Celia's throat tightened. He sounded so very weary, so very sad. 'But if my daughter is to face these consequences, then I wish to share them with her.'

A faint smile appeared on the Duke's finely featured face. 'Spoken like a good father,' he remarked. 'You will get your wish, Doctor, if it is to be so.'

Without another word, Dr Tedeschi bowed and retreated, while Dr Leone and the Duke discussed plans for the night.

Ned hadn't understood every word, but enough to get the gist, to know the danger they were in, even if they succeeded in getting into the Montemoro palace and confronting the Countess. For there was no way, Ned thought fiercely, that he, at any rate, would abandon the Tedeschis to the unjust ruling of the Duke. Suddenly, he remembered that play by Shakespeare he'd seen at the Globe, the one set around Shylock the Jewish moneylender, and his merciless bargain with the merchant Antonio. It seemed that the position was reversed here, he thought sadly, for the quality of mercy was strained indeed, in the person of the Duke. . . .

They left the Ducal Palace both more and less hopeful than when they'd started out. But Dr Leone was inclined to the former.

'You must not worry too much, Jacob,' he told the doctor in English as the gondola slid swiftly through the water. 'I am sure the Duke is a fair man. He would not imprison your daughter on a whim. And he has no love for the Montemoros. Far from it. I'm sure he believes they are guilty. But he has to move carefully. The Montemoros may not have the support of the Council of Ten any more, but there may still be some residual loyalty there. The present Count's father was on the Council, you know, even if the son is not highly regarded. And the

Duke cannot be seen to be directly crossing the Ten, or attempting to seize emergency powers. Otherwise he could be accused of acting like a dictator—and be overthrown. It has happened before, to other Dukes. He must proceed carefully. I think he sees an opportunity here to nail the Montemoros; but he must cover his own back too.'

'Oh, I know that,' said Dr Tedeschi quietly. He looked down into the water. 'But it is an odd thing, never to feel quite at home in the world.'

Dr Leone looked uncomfortable. 'None of us feel's that, my friend. Not Jew, not Christian, not Moor either, I don't suppose. We are orphans of Eden, all of us.'

'Yes,' said Dr Tedeschi. 'I suppose you are right.'

Ned couldn't contain himself any longer. 'It doesn't seem right to me at all that Sarah should be punished for being brave. Is there no justice in Venice?'

'Ned—' began Dr Leone, but Celia broke in indignantly.

'Ned's right. She has done nothing wrong. She should be protected, not punished.'

'She *won't* be punished,' said Dr Leone rather too heartily.

'Sarah has never seen herself as a pawn to be disposed of at leisure,' said Dr Tedeschi gently. 'That was a mistake of mine, allowing her to grow up thinking she might be able to move the pieces of her own life. It is not to be. It will never be, for people like us.'

'That's not true,' Ned burst out. 'We won't allow it,

Dr Tedeschi. We'll protect you and Sarah. We won't let them—'

Dr Tedeschi smiled sadly at him. 'You are a kind young man,' he said, 'and you have a true heart. But in this world, true hearts do not always win. That is the way of the world. That has always been the way.'

'Oh, tosh,' said Dr Leone roughly. 'You are far too gloomy, all of you. I am sure that this plan will work—the Montemoros will be quite undone and Sarah will be the heroine of the moment. You wait and see!'

Nobody had the heart to answer him.

Back at the house, Mistress Quickly came out to meet them. She looked anxious. 'It's Edmund,' she said. 'He's getting agitated. He kept asking for Beatrice. I had to soothe him several times.'

'I should have stayed with him,' said Dr Tedeschi. 'I'll go and have a look at him right away.'

'He's a good man,' said Dr Leone, looking after the doctor. 'I only wish . . . Ah well, let us not sadden ourselves with these things. Everything will turn out well. Dear Mistress Quickly, the Duke has agreed to help us. Tonight we will beard the Countess in her den and make her disgorge her prey. It will be a fine thing indeed!'

Ned and Celia looked at each other. Ned said gently, 'I'd best go to Murano straight away and let the others know.' He paused. 'Celia, will you do me the honour of coming with me?'

'Just try and stop me,' said Celia brightly, with a determined tilt of the chin. Nobody tried to stop her. They all knew better.

'Celia,' said Ned a little while later, 'there's something I want to say to you.'

They were sitting in the boat on the way to Murano. Sitting side by side, but not quite touching, suddenly shy with each other, but glad to be together.

Celia swallowed. She looked away, glancing at the boatman, who seemed oblivious to them. Ned said quietly, 'Something I've been wanting to say for a long time, Celia.' He put a hand gently on one of hers and withdrew it almost at once. 'Will you hear me?'

Celia wanted to speak, to say something pert or tart, or anything at all, but the bright words that usually came so readily to her lips had dried up in her mouth. Her heart beat fast. She felt almost scared. She looked at Ned, then away quickly. She nodded.

'I love you, Celia,' he said simply. 'I've loved you for a long time.' All those words he'd rehearsed, all the golden phrases, and yet what came to his lips was this simple declaration. 'And I wanted to know if perhaps you might . . .' He trailed off, suddenly losing courage, thinking: *What a fool I am, deluding myself into thinking that the look in her eyes back at the house meant somehow she shared my feelings. Now she'll be embarrassed, annoyed, and I've spoiled everything between us and . . .*

Then she turned her head and looked him right in the eyes. She faltered, 'I think . . . I think that I might, Ned. Oh, I think that I might!' And all of a sudden she was in his arms; so suddenly, in fact, that the boat rocked and the boatman called out in alarm. But his shouts turned to beaming smiles as he saw the young couple in each other's arms, kissing, and he shook his head happily, murmuring in Venetian dialect to himself, then turned back to his pole.

After a breathless moment, Celia drew back, laughing. 'Oh, Ned, I never would have thought it of you!'

'Thought what?' he said, laughing a little too, looking at Celia—his beautiful Celia—remembering the feel of her lips on his.

'That you could be such a good kisser,' she said pertly.

'Really?' he growled, and catching her up, kissed her again. 'And why would you think that?'

'Oh, I don't know,' she answered, dimpling up at him, her heart racing. 'I suppose I just don't have enough imagination. I never dreamed gruff, grumpy Ned would ever want to do anything like that!'

'Then you were wrong. On both counts,' retorted Ned, and the happiness hummed so loudly in his veins that he thought it must be heard. 'I am very interested in kissing . . . you,' he added, leaning towards her, 'and what's more, I am neither gruff nor grumpy but just mad about you and sure you wouldn't give a brass coin for me.'

'Oh, I don't know,' she said. 'Maybe I might not give a brass coin—but perhaps you might accept some other denomination?'

'That depends what it is,' said Ned, the back of his neck prickling with delight, 'and whether it is of sufficiently high coinage to—'

'Silly,' she said, and kissed him hard while the boatman grinned from his perch and the shore of Murano got closer and closer.

'Oh, Celia!' Ned said at last. 'What do you think your father will say, when he knows?'

'Fancy worrying about Father now,' she scolded happily, 'when you know he can be won over to my way of thinking any day of the week! Besides, he likes you.'

'Yes, but he *loves* you,' said Ned seriously. 'And he wants you to be happy. He won't want his only child affianced to a man who is not worthy to—'

'Don't be a fool,' said Celia briskly, her eyes sparkling. 'I can put up with a lot from you, Ned, but not that kind of nonsense.'

Ned laughed. 'And I can put up with anything, as long as you love me!'

'Then I have more to scold you with,' she said, and her voice softened. 'Ned, you dear, dear fool—you could have been killed if you'd had that duel with Henri. And for what? For what?'

'For stupid pride,' said Ned honestly. Then he grinned.

'But it might not have been me that was killed. I'm not such a bad swordsman, you know.'

'Really! Why would you want to kill Henri! He never did you any harm!'

'No, he didn't,' said Ned. 'I'm glad we never had the duel. He's not such a bad fellow, after all. Things do work out for the best sometimes, Celia.'

'Yes,' she said as the boat docked. Her chest constricted. 'And I hope they do now too, Ned. For Sarah, I mean.'

He nodded, suddenly sober. 'I fear it could go wrong, my love. But we must try. You understand, don't you?'

'You know I do,' she said as he helped her out of the boat, her hand resting in his as if it had always been meant. 'We must help them. What else can we do? Besides, why should we let ourselves be beaten by a bunch of unjust Venetian grandees?'

'That's the spirit,' he said, smiling. 'You know, darling, she reminds me of you.'

'Who?'

'Sarah Tedeschi. She's beautiful, clever, brave—and stubborn. Just like you.'

Celia glanced coquettishly up at him. 'Just as long as you haven't made a declaration of love to her too, Ned Fletcher!'

'Celia!' cried Ned. 'You really are the limit! How could you say such a silly thing? You'll like her, I know you will!'

'We'll see about that,' she answered, laughing at his vehemence, and took his arm as they walked away from the quay.

Three of Claudio's friends were already at the Murano house when Ned and Celia arrived. They were men as battle-hard and wary as Claudio, and they listened carefully to what Celia told them about the scene in the Duke's palace. Claudio's face darkened as she spoke.

'You do not have to concern yourselves,' he said grimly. 'Whatever happens, the Duke's men will not be allowed to arrest Sarah.' He did not explain quite what he would do, but Celia thought he would give his last drop of blood for the girl.

'We will be in position at nightfall,' Claudio went on. 'Sarah will be coming after us in a gondola on her own. She will insist on being taken to the same room where the patient lay. We know exactly where that is.'

Celia glanced at Sarah. Despite what she'd said earlier, she had taken to the other girl from the start. There was no haughtiness about Sarah and no false shyness, but determination and courage. *And despite what Ned said, she's more beautiful than me,* thought honest Celia; *a striking, unusual beauty, of the sort that makes men tremble and dream. The kind that painters want to paint and poets immortalize in verse. The sort men go to war for . . .* But just at the moment, Sarah seemed a little uncertain, as if the thing she'd wanted for so long—vindication of her good name and a chance to refute her accuser—had come upon her unexpectedly and she wasn't sure how to react.

Sarah must have felt her glance, for she turned and said, 'You have seen my father and my aunt. How have they borne my . . . my absence?'

'Quite well, considering,' said Celia a little drily. Then, relenting, she added, 'I think they believe you to be a queen, do you see, not a pawn.'

Sarah's eyes widened. 'A what? . . . Oh, I see.' She gave a faint smile. 'I am fortunate in my family.' She added, 'So are you, I think, Celia.'

Celia looked over at Ned and her father, who was joining animatedly in the discussion with Claudio. She said softly, 'I think I am too.'

'Signore Fletcher, he is the friend of your heart, no? You are to be married?'

'I hope so. One day,' said Celia, her heart pounding, looking over at Ned. 'What of you and Captain Battaglia?'

Sarah started and flushed.

'Come, girl, you can see he's head over heels for you,' said Celia with a grin. 'I don't suppose he's dared to breathe a word of it to you—he's much too afraid.'

'Afraid?' said the other girl, drawing herself up. 'But Claudio is the bravest and the kindest and most honourable man in all of Venice!'

'Quite,' said Celia. 'But bravery in those things doesn't equal bravery in love. He is a humble man, your Claudio, despite his fearsome looks.'

'There is nothing fearsome about Claudio,' said Sarah softly, 'except when he is facing evil. Then he will move heaven and earth to fight it.'

'When it's for your good, as well, I rather think,' said Celia gently.

She would have said more, but was interrupted at that moment by Ned. 'I will be going with them,' he said, and his eyes were like stars. 'Claudio has asked me to join them and I have agreed.'

'But that is danger—' Celia began before she could stop herself. Then she checked her words, tried to smile, and said, 'Very well, then. And I will go with Sarah.'

Ned stared at the two girls. But it was Sarah who said, in her stumbling English, 'You go me, Celia? But . . . Why?'

'Because I think you need someone with you. And because it will puzzle the Countess. She does not know me. She is less likely to just attack you if I'm there.' She grinned. 'And besides, I may know a few little tricks to loosen her tongue.'

'Celia!' protested Ned. 'That's far too danger—'

She put a finger to his lips. 'Shh. You'll be there with the other lads, just outside. And the Duke's men will be on the other side of the door. There's no danger.' She looked at him, and he knew the meaning in her eyes. *If you love me, you'll understand why I must do this.*

He nodded. 'You must be careful, then.'

She shrugged. 'Of course. I do not intend to court death just yet.'

'You very kind,' said Sarah. Her eyes were very bright, as if from unshed tears.

'Nonsense,' said Celia hastily. 'I'm just not about to be left out of things again. Once was enough. Isn't that right, Ned?'

'Quite right,' he said, smiling.

GHOSTS

Nightfall. It was a dark night, but all along the Grand Canal the lanterns of hurrying gondolas lit up the water, like fireflies dancing on glass. The soft glow of candlelight in the houses and flares along the waterfront turned the Canal into an enchanted world, full of sudden shadows and blazing beauty.

Wrapped in her cloak, Celia sat beside Sarah in the boat, one hand in the other girl's. Sarah's hand was rather cold, but it didn't tremble. She had hardly spoken a word the whole journey.

The gondolier was Claudio himself, dressed in the plain homespun of a boatman. He too had not spoken a word, but Celia could feel the tension from them both like a tangible thing. She thought: *This is an adventure for me; but for them, it's a matter of life and death. So much could go wrong. And even if it does not—if everything turns out for the best in all things, if the Countess is unmasked as a double-dyed villain and Sarah fully vindicated, then what?* There would be no great honour for her; she would be left free and unmolested, and that was all. Free to go back to the Ghetto with her father and to live the precarious life of a Jew in Venice, hemmed in between two bridges, at the mercy of the goodwill of their Christian lords. And what of Claudio? He would still be a poor, scarred ex-soldier, a Christian in love with a Jew. Of course, Sarah could convert to Christianity, but somehow Celia doubted that she'd want to. She loved her father and her aunt. She would see it as a betrayal of them. And Claudio would not be the kind of man to insist on it, or even perhaps to suggest it. For he respected Dr Tedeschi, who had treated his friend when no other doctor would.

Equally, it would be unthinkable for Claudio to convert. So it was an impossible conundrum. These two would have to part. Celia didn't want to imagine the pain and suffering that would cause. She wished with all her heart that somehow, there could be a solution. That somehow Sarah, her family, and her lover could live in peace and harmony and love and honour for the rest of their lives . . .

Just then Claudio whispered, 'We are near Ca' Montemoro. Are you ready, Sarah? Celia?'

'Yes,' said Sarah on a breathy sigh. But her hand in Celia's had started to shake a little now. Celia squeezed it.

'We're ready, Claudio,' she said boldly. 'And don't worry, I'll take good care of her.'

'Then I am glad,' he said simply. But Sarah said nothing at all.

He rowed along for a short while longer, till they could see the bulk of the great house, then drew up as a small boat approached them. A man in a guard's uniform called to them, 'Who goes there?'

'Visitors for the Countess Montemoro,' said Celia when Sarah still did not speak. 'There was a message sent this afternoon. She is expecting us.'

'Very well,' said the guard. 'Draw level with me, boatman. The ladies are to come in my craft to the palace. You are to leave. Those are Captain Maffei's orders.'

'Very well, sir,' said Claudio. But as he stepped down to help the girls out from his boat and into the other, Celia saw that his face was set in a rictus of anxiety. There was nothing she could do to reassure him now, though, for she herself had been suddenly stricken by unease. The Countess was not a fool and, if the stories about her were true, was ruthless into the bargain. What did they think they were doing, trying to trap someone like her?

She saw Sarah's face clearly as the girl took Claudio's hand and stepped from their gondola into the guard's boat. It was very pale, the eyes very bright. Sarah's and Claudio's eyes met. And in that instant Celia knew, with a leap of the heart, that Claudio was not loving in vain. He saw it too, and his face changed, softened, a look of incredulous joy coming into his eyes.

The guard groused, 'Hurry up, fellow, the Countess doesn't like to be kept waiting.'

'Yes,' said Claudio hastily, and in a trice first Sarah, then Celia were in the guard's boat. The guard was just about to row away when Sarah said breathlessly, 'Is there a place the gondolier can tie up his boat to wait for us for the return journey? He gave us a very fair price for this trip, and I should very much like not to be bothered with having to find another boatman when our business is finished.'

'Someone from the house could take you back—' began the guard.

'I should not dream of disturbing them. And this gondolier is honest, unlike so many others. Such a one should be encouraged, do you think not, Officer?' she said, smiling up at him so dazzlingly that the guard was quite overcome.

He muttered, 'I suppose that is true. Hey, fellow,' he shouted at Claudio, who was waiting by impassively, 'get yourself over to that landing-stage there. Wait for us. Your fares might be a while. I just don't know how long. We weren't told.'

'Yes, your honour,' said Claudio, ducking his head in a humble gesture. 'And thank you, sweet lady,' he said to Sarah, his voice changing. 'I shall wait. I shall wait for you all night. For ever, if need be.'

'Hey, fellow, fancy yourself as a gallant, do you?' said the guard with a hoot of laughter. 'Young ladies who call on countesses are a little above your league, I would say.' And still laughing, he rowed away from Claudio, towards the lights of the palace glowing before them.

Meanwhile, directly on the other side of the canal, in the shadow of a dark alley between two houses, a huddle of figures waited for Claudio's signal. Amongst them was Ned. Next to him was Henri. The young Frenchman had found out what was planned and had immediately declared that the best sword in Paris was certainly not going to stay in its scabbard tonight if any game was to be had. So he had been coopted into the plan and included in the invasion party of Claudio's men.

The invasion party must be one of young, fit men, so Master Ashby and Dr Leone had gone back to the Ducal Palace to meet with the Duke's men. Dr Leone would have preferred to go with Claudio's men, but reluctantly agreed that, as a friend of the Duke's, he must be the go-between and Ashby must come with him, for he was certainly no fighting man. But Dr Tedeschi, his sister Rachel, Mistress Quickly, and the poor madman Edmund stayed at Dr Leone's house. The first three would have come too but had to watch over the fourth, who could scarcely be asked to fight alongside his former comrades, but had to be guarded, in case he should do himself a mischief, wandering around the streets searching for his Beatrice again.

'There it is!' said Henri as his sharp eyes made out a light moving up, down, up, down, three times. 'It's coming from the Ca' Montemoro watergate.'

Claudio's second-in-command, a thick-set young man called Lucius, barked an order. The men scrambled to the small boats waiting under the poles of the landing-stage at the end of the alley. They set off without lights, navigating under the sure guidance of Lucius, who knew the canal like the back of his hand. They reached the other side without incident, one or two houses up from Ca' Montemoro; then one by one the boats slipped closer and closer to the landing-stage where Claudio sat waiting.

There were no guards about. Claudio whispered to them that there had been one there just a few minutes ago, but he'd been called inside, Henri translated to Ned, on some 'urgent matter.' Claudio looked rather grim as he spoke, and Ned knew he must be worried for his beloved—as indeed he was for his, though not as much, perhaps. Not because he cared less, but because he knew his Celia better than Claudio did his Sarah, and thought she might be a match even for a wily and ruthless aristocratic woman.

Clearly, anyhow, the Countess did not expect any attack from the outside—no, the danger was inside, and she must think she was close to dealing with it. For the message that had been sent to the palace on Sarah's behalf had made it quite clear that the girl had information that she was willing to trade for safe passage out of the city for herself and her family. The Countess must think it would be easy to shut her up for good—or even, at the best, to bribe her handsomely to stay away and keep her mouth shut.

Ned was jerked from his thoughts by a soft exclamation from Claudio. 'Look!' He was pointing to an arched window on the second floor where, just for an instant, something white had fluttered. *Celia's handkerchief,* thought Ned with his pulse racing. *They're in the room, with the Countess.*

The Countess was dressed all in black now, as if she were in mourning. Only her ruff was white, and it stood up around her face, which had been powdered so it was no longer sallow but almost as white as the ruff. It made her look like a ghost. When she entered, her cold blue eyes settled on Sarah at once, her gaze flicking over Celia with little interest. But it was to Celia she spoke first.

'You are English. What have you to do with this business?'

'I am a courtier of our Queen's,' lied Celia boldly, 'and I am here to tell you that our monarch's protection is extended to this young woman and that, as soon as is practicable, she shall be moved to England, where her father is to take up a post of doctor to the royal household.'

'Indeed!' said the Countess with an arch of her eyebrow. 'You speak good Italian, for an Englishwoman. Pray, remind me, what is your name?'

'Emilia Lanier,' said Celia, using the name that had been written in the message. 'English by birth, but Venetian by ancestry. My father was a Bassano.'

'A Bassano!' said the Countess with great scorn. 'Converted Jews, it's said. No wonder you take this girl's part.'

'My father's family is close to the Duke's,' said Celia warningly, 'as my husband's is to the English Queen.'

The Countess shrugged. 'Very well. So—you are the one that boy who came to visit my husband was really working for.'

'Yes,' said Celia.

'I knew the kidnap story was a lie. So, you are here now as her guard, are you? In case I should go back on my word of safe passage. You fool—do you not think it is easy enough to disappear even such as you? If an English courtier is foolish enough to go in a boat a little merry and fall overboard, then that is sad, but not such an unusual thing.' She came close to Celia. Her eyes were like blue ice. 'So do not think you can threaten me, girl. I hold real power—not the gossamer kind that can be destroyed in an instant.' She turned to Sarah. 'Enough of this. What have you come to say, Jewish witch?'

'That I am no witch, though indeed I am Jewish,' said the girl, her head held high. All trace of fear had left her face now and only a cold anger burned there. 'That you are a corrupt, evil woman who has sought to silence me because you thought I knew about the ugly reality behind your façade of respectability. You fool, when you accused me I knew nothing. Nothing at all. But now—now I know everything.'

'Indeed?' said the Countess, her face impassive. 'And what is this thing you think you know?'

Sarah's eyes glittered. '*You* are in league with the Verona trader Gamboretto. Indeed, you are not just in league with him, you direct his operations. It is *you,* not he, who finances his evil schemes. It is you who skims off the profits of his corruption. It is you who waits in the shadows like a giant spider bloated with blood, as sailors are slaughtered on the high seas, and valuable cargoes are lost, and merchants and their workers lose their livelihoods as you destroy their trade. It is you who is at the heart of one of the biggest and ugliest of corrupt enterprises in all of Venice—nay, even beyond. You are behind this evil plague of piracy. And you have profited very well from theft and corruption and mass murder.'

Celia stared at her. Sarah had spoken as if she had

proof. Real proof. She had taken a very big risk, gambled big. Would it pay off?

The Countess's face had gone very still. Her eyes were like slits in the white mask of her face. But her voice was calm enough as she said after a little silence, 'What a thrilling tale you spin, to be sure. Piracy! Evil schemes! Corruption! Mass murder! Why, my dear, you make me out to be some kind of evil genius.'

'Perhaps that is what you are,' said Sarah. Her colour was very high. 'It is a game with high stakes you play. And though some can play such games, others can't. And that's what you're afraid of. That's why you've been persecuting me with your accusations, why you wanted to find me at all costs. You were afraid someone had told me about it. Someone who has been caught up in this scheme, because he can't stop you and never has been able to. Someone who's enjoyed the money your schemes bring, but never the risk, unlike you. Someone who knows that the Duke's secret police have started to suspect that something is very rotten indeed in the house of Montemoro. Someone who may even be filled with remorse at what has been happening, whose sleep is troubled by the last screams of dying sailors. Someone who doesn't have a strong stomach and nerves of steel, like you.'

'Oh, yes?' said the Countess. She crossed to the door. 'Captain Maffei, will you come in?'

The grizzled officer must have been standing just behind the door, for he came in at once. Celia shot an anguished glance at Sarah.

'Captain Maffei, I want you here as a witness. Shut the door. Yes. Come in. I want you to listen to what this girl has to say. She is accusing this house—and me—of corruption and piracy and murder and all kinds of evil.'

'Oh, my lady,' said the officer in a deep, impassive voice, 'that is a wicked thing for her to say. Why should she say such wicked things?'

His eyes—very bright, very light brown—rested speculatively on the two girls for an instant. Celia shivered. With his strong features, his hawk nose and intent, blank eyes, the man had something of the air of a bird of prey. An ageing bird of prey, perhaps, but just as dangerous as in youth and twice as merciless.

'I think the little Jew believes she has someone to back her up in this wickedness, someone she has spellbound to do her bidding. Can you think who that might be, Maffei?'

She is playing with us, thought Celia, suddenly horrified. *She is playing with us like a cat plays with a mouse. She has an ace up her sleeve—something we don't suspect, not at all.*

'My lady,' said the man respectfully, 'I am not privy to such dark thoughts, but if I may hazard a guess—it is perhaps a ghost, a sadly departed soul, one who has been frail for quite some time and for whom we mourn even this very hour.'

'Stop this,' said Sarah jerkily. 'You don't frighten me. You know to whom I refer—not to the poor woman my father treated, who may well have died; she was frail, that's true—but to your husband, madam. To the Count!'

'But, my dear,' said the Countess without missing a beat, 'it is to him that we refer. My poor husband, the Count, who in a fit of sadness and depression took poison in his room this very afternoon. Poison, in a cup of sweet wine. Is it not sad?'

Celia and Sarah stared at her. Then Sarah quavered, 'You . . . you killed him. You killed your own husband, because you were afraid he might talk. . . .'

'Everyone knew the balance of his mind was disturbed,' said the Countess coolly. 'He was falling to pieces. He was capable of any rashness. It had been so for some time, hadn't it, Maffei? From the time you'—she pointed a long index finger at Sarah—'you put a wicked spell on him to make him so besotted with you that he could think of nothing else but you and called your name in his sleep. . . .'

Sarah had gone as white as a sheet. 'No,' she said, taking a step back. 'No. That's not true. It's not true. It started because he asked me if I knew Verona—and it meant nothing to me then, but it does now.'

'And you thought that meant he was about to confide in you, about Gamboretto and the pirates?' The

Countess looked supremely confident. 'You fool. You still don't understand, do you? The Count closed his eyes and ears to Gamboretto and to all that entailed. Remorse? Sleep troubled by sailor's dying screams? Not a bit of it. My husband liked the good things our . . . our association with these men brings. As long as I had the contact with the actual organizing of it—and not him—he could pretend it wasn't really happening.' Her tone held a hint of bitterness. 'It's always been that way.'

Sarah stammered, 'But—but the secret police—they were on your track, they might have found out, in time. . . .'

The Countess shrugged. 'They had not ever come close. They knew very little. Only rumours. I know, because we had an informer in their ranks. They could not touch us. No. Verona meant something quite other to him.' She looked at Celia. 'I overheard him talking to your messenger boy, that fool of an Englishman. Pleading with him to take a commission. And I knew then I couldn't trust him any more. His sentiments had got the better of him. He was always an unstable man, and now he was a liability. I knew I couldn't trust him in anything any more—not even about Gamboretto, eventually.'

Sarah was very pale. 'But I don't understand. . . . I don't . . .'

The Countess had a strange smile on her face. 'Then you shall. Everyone should know the truth before they die. What else did he ask you, that fateful night? Do you remember, my pretty witch?'

'Don't, Sarah,' said Celia. 'Don't answer.'

But Sarah stared at the Countess, like a little bird mesmerized by a snake. She quavered, 'He asked about my father and my mother.'

The Countess began to laugh. 'Of charity, lady, what kin are you? What countryman? What name? What parentage? And what of Verona? Ah, Captain Maffei, is it not a good joke!'

'Yes, my lady,' he said, though his face was very grim and very dark.

The Countess reached inside her dress and pulled out a tiny locket. She said, 'I found it on him, at the very last. He died with her face on his heart.' She sighed. 'I believe he knew what that cup of wine contained and he drank it willingly. He wanted to die. Thus do fools pass away.'

She clicked open the locket. And there, inside, was the painted miniature of a beautiful young woman, with creamy skin, large, long-lashed dark eyes, and dark red hair.

'Oh, my God!' said Celia, staring at the painted face, then at the other girl, as the full force of the revelation burst in on her. For Sarah was the spitting image of the young woman in the portrait. 'Oh, my God, no, it cannot be. . . .'

The Countess smiled. It was a wintry smile that froze

her features into a cold mask. 'She was a scheming little creature from Verona. Her name was Julietta. My husband . . . he was always a fool. He had had many women in the past. He kept mistresses. It did not bother me, for they meant nothing to him. But this one—this one was different. He was besotted, mad with love. She became pregnant. Pregnant with you, girl. Well. He was afraid of my reaction. So he hid her while she was with child. He thought he should hide it completely from me and that once the child was safely born he would seek an annulment of his marriage to me, on the grounds of my barrenness.' Her eyes flashed. 'The ungrateful, weak, unreliable fool that he was! I'd given him everything, I'd risked my neck for him—and he still sought to rid himself of me. But I found out his secret. I found her. And I found her child. . . .' Her eyes glittered, her hands shaped into claws. 'I arranged for Julietta's death, her disposal and that of her baby. It was done quietly. He never knew. He thought she'd left him—I arranged for a note to be left at the safe house, saying the child had been born dead and that she couldn't bear disappointing him and had gone away. He was beside himself, searched for her—but in the end, he believed it. There were no witnesses, you see, except for Maffei and the hired man. And they didn't talk.'

'There was one other,' said Maffei grimly. 'By cursed bad luck, there was a witness that night on the canal. Someone saw us, heard us with the baby. And so . . .'

'Even then we were fortunate,' said the Countess, and over her features spread a ghastly parody of a smile. 'You see, this witness was a silly young woman, an acquaintance of my family, who came to me in great distress with the information, having no idea at all of course that I was involved. It was easy to silence her.' She paused. 'Strangely enough, I had a child of my own only a year or so later. The Count could no longer say I was barren. He did not love me or our daughter—but he could not forsake me any longer. And over the years he'd grown used to my fortune, to his easy life. He bent to my will happily enough. And so you see, everything worked for the best for me.' Her eyes glittered. 'Until . . . until the cursed night that my husband walked into this room where you sat—and saw you looking at him with *her* eyes.'

'No,' said Sarah, taking a step back. 'No. No. It's not true! My father is Dr Tedeschi! I was born in the Ghetto, brought up in the Ghetto. You are lying! Lying!'

'I wish I were,' said the Countess quietly. 'Maffei, tell her.'

'We disposed of mother and child separately,' said the officer, looking at Sarah with his unblinking yellow stare. 'It was safer that way. I killed the woman myself, but I hired a man to drown the newborn in the lagoon. I thought he had done as he was told. But now I recall there was a squeamishness in him, though he swore he would do it. The canal where I met him—where that fool of a girl saw us—was not so far from the Ghetto. He must have left the babe there.'

'Like Moses in the bulrushes,' said the Countess. 'Except in reverse—Pharaoh's child, left with Moses's people. That's what the witness saw, you see. Maffei and the other man and the baby. What's the trouble, child? You stand like a statue. Is it that you still do not believe? I would force that traitor to tell you the truth, but I cannot, for he died many years ago and he never talked of what he'd done—cared too much for his own skin, I'd say. If I'd known that he'd not killed the baby . . .' She smiled, showing all her teeth. 'So the good doctor never told you of your true origins and that you were a foundling, eh? That's another good joke.' She began to laugh. 'The stars have truly conspired against you and for me, have they not, girl? Is yours not a piteous and strange fate? For you are not Moses's child, but Pharaoh's. And you died twice—on the day you were born and today.' She made a sign to Maffei. 'Take her down you know where. We will finish tonight what should have been done sixteen years ago.'

'No!' shouted Celia, throwing herself in front of Sarah. But the officer just thrust her aside with a rough shove that sent her sprawling to the ground. In an instant, the Countess was on her, holding her down, while Maffei seized the unresisting Sarah and dragged her away, through the door into the little room nearby. Celia heard a creak, a thump, then silence.

At that moment, there was a commotion in the corridor outside: shouts, yells, the clash of steel. The Countess started and Celia instantly seized her opportunity. Scrambling up, she made a dash for the room where Sarah and Maffei had disappeared.

It was a storeroom, just as Dr Tedeschi had said. But in the middle of the floor was a trapdoor. And it was ajar, revealing a ladder underneath and a dark passageway.

But Celia didn't get time to start down the ladder after them. Shrieking imprecations, the Countess was on her, a dagger in her hands, a mad look in her eyes. Celia fought desperately, knowing that the Countess would kill her without regard for the consequences. She could hear the clash of steel outside and knew that her friends were on their way. But the guards must be putting up a stiff resistance. Her friends might be too late to save her and Sarah.

Suddenly, the Countess got her hand free of Celia's grasp. She lunged with the dagger, striking for the heart. Celia ducked, but not quite in time. The knife caught her hard in the left arm. Blood spurted out.

A terrible pain gripped Celia and she fell. She expected to die then and prepared to defend her life fiercely, despite the hideous pain of her stabbed arm. But the commotion was growing louder, closer.

The Countess must have decided she had no time. In

a trice she had scrambled down the ladder and disappeared, slamming the trapdoor shut behind her.

Celia tried to crawl to it, to open it again, to follow her. But the pain was too much. She fainted.

The next thing she knew was Ned's agonized voice in her ear. 'Oh, my darling, my darling, I'll never forgive myself, never, oh, my sweet, I knew I should never have left you to—'

'Stop it,' she croaked, opening her eyes and looking into his terrified face. 'I'm not dead yet.'

'Oh, thank God, thank God,' he cried. 'Oh, darling Celia, I was so frightened! You've blood all over. I thought . . .'

'It's just a flesh wound, I think, but it hurts,' she said, trying to sit up, with his help. She put a hand on her wound, trying to staunch the bleeding. Ned quickly tore a sleeve off his shirt and wound it around her arm to form a bandage. She tried to smile. 'Your poor shirt, it'll never be the same again.'

Claudio burst in, drawn sword in hand. It was covered in blood too—but not his. His face was grim as he took in the situation. He said, *'Sarah.'*

'Down there,' said Celia, pointing to the trapdoor. 'There's a ladder. Maffei and the Countess, they've taken her. I don't know where it leads.'

Claudio didn't say any more, but threw open the trapdoor and disappeared at once down the ladder.

Celia said, 'You should go with him, Ned. I would, but I can't, not like this.'

'I don't want to leave you,' he said. 'The Countess . . .'

'Is gone. She killed the Count. Poisoned him.'

'But why? Did he confess?'

'No. It wasn't what we thought. Sarah . . . Sarah's his natural daughter. Verona—that's where she came from.'

Ned was understandably bewildered. 'What? Who?'

'Sarah's mother. Her real mother. Who had an affair with the Count, years ago.'

'Then Dr Tedeschi . . .'

'Is her adoptive father. Yes.'

At that moment, Henri burst into the room, followed by Lucius and another of Claudio's friends. 'We've routed them all,' he declared, then checked himself when he saw Celia. 'What did they do to you?'

'Don't worry about me,' said Celia. 'Ned's here. You go down there, Henri. Claudio's going to need you. The Countess and Maffei have got Sarah.'

'They won't get far. The Duke's men are coming, at last,' said Henri. 'I saw them coming down the canal. They should be here any moment.'

'A little late to hear anything,' said Celia, stricken, as the young Frenchman went down the ladder after the others. 'Oh, Ned! The Countess confessed everything to us—the piracy; the murder of her husband; the murder of his mistress, long ago; the attempted murder of his child; even the murder of some poor anonymous witness who came to her for help. She's a monster, a monster! And now they'll have heard nothing and she'll get away with it!'

'She won't get away with much,' said Ned quietly, 'not if Claudio has anything to say about it. And there's your wounding to explain, Celia . . . and the Duke will listen, I'm sure of it.'

Celia was about to protest that the Countess had always had the Devil's own luck, when suddenly they both jumped out of their skins as a frightful shriek tore the night. Ned jumped up. 'It's from outside!' he cried. 'Outside, on the canal! The Duke's men! I told you, Celia!'

He helped Celia to her feet and together they hobbled into the next room, to the window that looked out onto the water. And there, in the light of the flares of the landing-stage, they saw something they would never forget.

Nemesis

A dripping-wet creature emerged from the canal, a tall, ghostly figure with hair that shone with an unearthly glow in the light of the flares. With another of those inhuman shrieks, it sprang onto the landing-stage, straight in the path of the two figures who stood there frozen for one fatal instant. The Countess and Maffei had clearly been about to jump into their waiting boat, but just for that instant, they fell back. Maffei shouted something, a command to move; the sodden figure stopped, turned, stared at him, its eyes wide, anguished, mad.

Then without warning, it leaped for the man's throat. Taken by surprise, Maffei stumbled, tripped, went back against the side of the landing-stage. Even from the window, Ned and Celia could hear the crack of his skull. And then he fell off, tumbling into the water. He did not come up again. . . .

There were some boats on the water, fast approaching; people shouting. The Duke's men. But they were still a little distance away. Out of the corner of his eye Ned saw someone jump from one of the boats and start to swim towards the landing-stage . . .

. . . where the Countess was struggling with the figure. Celia saw her dagger flash, saw it come down. The Countess's assailant staggered, shouted, 'Beatrice, oh Beatrice, wait for me!'

The Countess laughed. Her laugh was as inhuman as the shriek had been. They saw her bend down and whisper something to the madman. Then she brought the dagger down again, to finish him off. But suddenly, the madman sprang up and grabbed her hand. The dagger clattered harmlessly on the landing-stage. Then the madman sprang, with the struggling Countess in his arms, straight from the landing-stage and into the water.

The swimmer reached the place instants later. Too late. The Countess and the madman were lost in the murky depths of the dark water and there was nothing anybody could do.

Wearily, the swimmer dragged himself up onto the

landing-stage, and Celia and Ned saw that it was Dr Tedeschi. He stood there with bowed head and dripping clothes as the Duke's boats approached and the men clambered out.

Celia and Ned looked at each other; then with one accord they made for the trapdoor. Gently, he helped her down the ladder. At the bottom was a long passageway and then stairs leading down, down to the bowels of the palace. There was an open door at the end, and when they went through it there was a little room, where they found Sarah and Claudio in each other's arms. Sarah was sobbing and Claudio was silent; his men were around them, standing guard.

Claudio looked at Ned and Celia over his beloved's head. He whispered, 'I let them get away, for it was the only way to save her.'

'They didn't get away,' said Celia between stiff lips. 'They didn't, because . . . because your friend, he stopped them. He killed them, Claudio, by sacrificing himself. He brought Nemesis on them. He avenged his love.'

'My friend?' said Claudio, staring at her with his black eyes all aglitter.

'Edmund,' said Celia. 'Poor Edmund, who longed so for his lost Beatrice. What happened to them, Claudio?'

'He loved her long ago, when he was very young,' said Claudio faintly. 'Beatrice was the daughter of the steward of the da Piero family, who were close to the Duke. The Countess was a da Piero, you know, before she married Montemoro. Beatrice's father did not approve of Edmund as a suitor, of course. Too poor, too foreign, too young. Edmund said they planned to run away from Venice together, for there was great danger for them here. He was never clear just what, but implied that they had seen something terrible one Carnival night, something that implicated someone very powerful. He thought it was the Duke, or possibly someone in his household. He didn't know who it was, really. He had never found out. He never dared.' He sighed. 'Edmund and Beatrice arranged to meet at the Rialto bridge one night. He waited, but she never came. She sent word she had changed her mind and would never see him again. A day later she died in a boating accident on the canal. Accident, some said. But others said she had taken her own life.'

'She did not,' said Celia slowly. 'She was murdered by a woman she thought was a friend. The Countess of Montemoro, who used to be a da Piero. The Countess, to whom in great distress she'd told what she'd seen at the canal. And tonight, somehow, Edmund knew that the Countess had murdered his lost love, his Beatrice.'

'But why? Why would she do such a thing?' whispered Claudio.

'Because Beatrice was witness to a terrible deed committed by the Countess long ago. She was witness to the attempted murder of a newborn child, with the suggestion its mother had been killed too. Poor girl!

How it must have preyed on her mind! She didn't know who was behind it and must have gone to the one person she thought she could trust. She must not even have told Edmund she was going to do it.'

'Poor Beatrice. Poor Edmund,' said Claudio sadly. 'He stayed away from Venice for years because of the memories. He got the mind-sickness only last year, after our last campaign. And he got it into his head then that he must return to Venice, that Beatrice had somehow miraculously escaped from her watery grave and that he must find her. I came back with him, because I could not let him go as he was. I tried to help him, to give him a home at my house, but he wouldn't stay. He said one day he would find her, and she would explain what had happened, and they would be happy together for ever.'

It was the longest speech Celia had ever heard him make, and when it was finished he sat there silently, his arm around his weeping love, his black eyes fixed on the past. That sad, grim past that had so strangely and so tightly bound the fates of his friend Edmund and his love, Sarah; that had destroyed Edmund's Beatrice and Sarah's mother, together. Beside one canal the fates of the doomed lovers had been sealed; beside another, at last, justice had been done; and now those poor lovers might rest in peace, together for ever, just as Edmund had hoped. But if the revelation of that past had at last destroyed the wicked people who had brought so much suffering to so many, and brought peace to his friend

Edmund's troubled soul, it had also erased Sarah's very sense of who she was. And Claudio felt the pain of that keenly, with every surge of his aching heart.

Celia and Ned left them then and went out of that room and through a low door that led, as they'd half expected, to the watergate and the landing-stage. Henri was out there with Dr Leone, Celia's father, and the Duke's men, all talking in low voices about what had just happened. When Dr Ashby saw Celia and Ned he came towards them, crying, 'Thank God you're both safe! Thank God!'

But Celia looked around for the other man who should have been there—the stooped, dripping swimmer who had come too late to stop Edmund wreaking a terrible justice on Maffei and the Countess. She saw him at last, slumped in a dark corner, his head in his hands. She went over to him and touched him gently on the shoulder, saying, 'Dr Tedeschi—your daughter is safe too. I can take you to her.'

He looked up at her, his eyes red with tears, and said, 'I am guilty. I have done wrong all these years. I have lied, because my poor departed wife and I loved her as soon as we found her, abandoned under the bridge that night, so many years ago. . . .'

'It was not a lie,' said Celia fiercely. 'You *are* her father. Your wife was her mother.'

'No,' said Dr Tedeschi. 'Tonight . . . Edmund—he told me. He was lucid, almost normal. He told me what he saw that long-ago night on the canal. He and his Beatrice. And I knew then—I knew who Sarah must be. I knew why the Countess was looking for her and why the Count was in such a state of nerves. I could not help it; the Montemoros' name escaped me then, in my distress. Then later he heard that was where Claudio had gone—and when we . . . when we set out in the boat, he insisted on coming. It was impossible to stop him. But oh, how I wish I had!'

'No, Dr Tedeschi,' said Celia gently. 'It was better he came—for he avenged his Beatrice in the end, and he avenged Sarah too, without knowing it.' And she sat down and told him all that had passed between the Countess and Sarah.

When she had finished, she took his hand, and said, 'Will you let me take you to her? For I think she needs her father more than ever now. And you *are* her father, in heart and soul. And that's what matters, Dr Tedeschi, even more than blood.'

He looked up at her, without speaking. Then he nodded and straightened his shoulders and got up. Only then did he seem to catch sight of the bandage on her arm, for he drew his breath and whispered, 'You are hurt, Celia.'

'Only a little, Doctor,' she said, smiling at him, 'and nothing that a good doctor like you won't make better very soon.'

'Yes, of course,' he said, faintly, and allowed himself to be led away.

The Lovers of Venice

The scandal of the Montemoros was one Venice would talk about for many years to come. The revelation of their corruption and wickedness shocked even the supposedly unshockable Venetians. The Council of Ten and the Duke decided, however, that only some things should come to light, so people got to hear about the dealings with Gamboretto and most things connected with that. It helped that no one in the present Council or in the present Duke's entourage had benefited from those crimes, so the house could be put in order without too much distress. Much of the Montemoro estate, including their Venetian palace, was seized to pay reparations to the victims of their piracy. But their neglected daughter, Isabella, was allowed to continue living in her uncle's house in Verona, which she had always regarded as her own home anyway.

The poisoning of the Count was hushed up as well: that was for the sake of Isabella, an innocent victim of her parents' machinations. The truth was too terrible to put on her shoulders. After the funeral she returned to the only family she knew, to build a new life and forget about the past.

Edmund's funeral was very different to the quiet, almost furtive ones of the Montemoros and Maffei. There was a brilliant ceremony in the church where he'd loved to shelter, with the angelic music playing, to sing him to his rest. The church was packed with mourners, including Beatrice's remorseful family; and he was laid to rest in the cemetery near her, so that in death, if not in life, the cruelly parted lovers could be together.

As to the revelation of Sarah's true parentage, and the lengths the Countess had gone to in order to hide it, this was kept completely quiet, at the express request of people to whom the Venetian state owed a good deal, and had indeed showed their gratitude by a rich purse of gold and precious stones. As there was nothing to be gained from such revelations, the request was granted.

But after the Council of Ten had met on the matter,

the Duke sent a letter to the Tedeschis: it had been decided that if they persisted in not revealing Sarah's true identity, and if Sarah persisted in refusing to accept the possibility of leaving her family, then the Tedeschis might be more comfortable in a place other than Venice, and should find a new home, far away from the city, where they would not be known. Or else Sarah, as the natural child of the Count, might be taken from them, to be reared a Christian and given in marriage to some man more suiting her station than a poor soldier. The Duke clearly indicated that the Council had been merciful in the matter and had kept the matter from the Inquisition; but if this body came to hear of it, there was no way the Tedeschis could be protected. They were no longer at home in the city in which they had lived for so long.

It wasn't just in the city generally. They were no longer at home in the Ghetto, for though their neighbours did not know the full extent of what had happened, still they knew, through Tartuffo's spiteful hints and through rumours sweeping the city, that the Tedeschis had had a hand in the undoing of the Montemoros. It did not make people feel comfortable; the way to survive, as a Jew, was to keep your head down and not become involved in the plots and machinations of outsiders. As to the people beyond the Ghetto, it made them feel uncomfortable too, and suspicious. Dr Tedeschi had lost nearly all of his patients, Jews and Christians. The few who came were gawkers, curious souls who hoped to find out more. They were usually sent packing by Rachel, who could not abide 'sniffers after sadness,' as she called them.

For it was indeed a sad house now. There was no doubt of the love between Sarah and her father and her aunt—but it was a love tempered now with the burden of knowledge, and must slowly be rebuilt into natural joy and warmth. And there was a question over the other great love of Sarah's life, her Claudio. How could they marry, when the laws of the land forbade it, unless Sarah gave up the only kin she knew in the world? For the time being, all that had been decided was that Claudio might visit her, in whichever city they might chance to go to, and that, in time, perhaps, something might be worked out. . . . Where they would go they had no real idea, and no stomach for thinking about it. They would wander where they could and try to find a crack in the world in which to hide.

The Ashbys and Ned and Dr Leone were frequent visitors to the house in the Ghetto that was shunned by everyone else. For a few days now Ned and Celia had been racking their brains trying to think of a solution for the family's woes. But the problem was too big for them. It was the weight of the world pressing down on their friends' shoulders, and try as they might, they could not budge it even a tiny fraction.

Soon they themselves would be gone. Back to their own lives in London. Back to safety and comfort and a glowing new future. For Ned had asked Master Ashby for Celia's hand and, rather to his surprise, the merchant hadn't turned him down flat. 'I want you to wait two years,' he said. 'You both need to grow up more, and if I am to make you an associate in the business as I wish to do—my future son-in-law cannot remain a mere clerk—I wish to make sure you understand it more. But I know Celia is very happy, and I want only her happiness. You are a good and clever lad, Ned, with a true heart, and I dare say you will never waver from her.'

'Oh, sir, you can be sure I never would! I would rather cut out my heart and throw it to the dogs! I would rather pierce my flesh with a thousand barbs! I—'

'I see the picture,' said Ashby hastily. 'You are a fortunate lad, for you have the love not only of Celia, but also of my sister, who told me quite roundly that if I dared to disapprove, she would personally make sure I would walk on hot coals for the rest of my life! No, don't look so worried, Ned,' he added, laughing. 'I did not need to be persuaded quite so harshly! You have my blessing on this enterprise, lad; really, you do.'

But poor Sarah and Claudio had no such blessing. Oh, it wasn't that Dr Tedeschi disapproved; his opinion of Claudio was very high. It was just that he was defeated by events, crushed by the world, unable to fight against fate. And their friends watched helplessly. Even Dr Leone's optimism seemed to have deserted him. Slowly, the Tedeschi family pieced together its possessions and made ready to leave Venice for ever. No one hurried them; even the city authorities understood. A strange kind of shame gripped people, but it was no good. What was said was said; what had to be done, had to be done. It would be ever thus, until the world changed.

It was the last day the Ashbys and Ned were in Venice. The last time they would see their friends. That afternoon, if the winds were still favourable, they would set sail and leave Venice. That morning the d'Arcys, father and son, had come to say goodbye. They were staying on in Venice a while longer before setting off back home. Many plans were made about meeting up again in Paris, or in London; for the families had become good friends now. Ned had a strong inkling that one day, perhaps, Jacques d'Arcy would be calling in at their house with more than a polite greeting for Bess Quickly, for his eyes were often on her, and hers on his.

As to Henri, he had met a young Venetian beauty by the name of Maria and was in no hurry to see the shores of his own country. He regaled Ned and Celia with stories of the beauty's stiff-necked family, and Ned, listening to his stories, recognized now the genuine wit, the humour, and the kind, observant spirit under the young Frenchman's light ways. *He is a fine man, and one I'm honoured to call friend,* he thought. *How stupid I was before! But then I had reason to be. I didn't know myself, or Celia's heart. Not like now . . .*

Celia caught his eye and smiled, in that way that made his toes tingle. She said softly, 'What are you thinking of, Ned?'

'Of you,' he answered, 'and how I wish our friends could be as happy as we are.'

'Yes,' she said sadly. 'If only wishes came true.'

'If only there were a place in the world to which they could go; some place where they could fly, like birds to their nests, and be happy, and—'

'Is there such a place?' said Henri, overhearing, and then suddenly the melancholy silence that fell on them when he spoke was suddenly broken with a yell as Dr Leone jumped to his feet, sending his chair crashing behind him, and boomed, 'In God's name, there is! What a blind fool I've been! Why didn't I think of it before!' And then, before any of the astonished company could ask him what on earth he was talking about, he strode out of the room and out of the house, slamming the front door behind him.

He didn't come back for hours. Matthew Ashby was getting worried, for the time for them to board their ship was getting closer and still his friend had not returned. The bags were packed, the porters ready; the post-chaises had drawn up outside the door. They could wait no longer.

Just as the Ashbys and Ned made their last goodbyes to the servants, a post-chaise came hurrying down the alley. From it tumbled Dr Leone. He was bright red, his hair standing up on end, but there was a beaming smile on his face. 'I'm sorry, my friends, I hope I'm not late. Are we ready to go to the quay, Mateo?'

'Of course. Where have you been?' snapped Ashby. 'We thought we should have to leave without saying goodbye.'

'Can't have that, oh, no!' shouted Dr Leone. 'Hop in, then; let's get to the quay.' And not a word would he tell them about where he'd been, or what he'd been doing, or anything else.

As on the day they'd arrived, the quay was thronged with people bustling to and fro: sailors, porters, dock workers, merchants, hot-food sellers, all sorts. Their ship was waiting for them, the gangplank in readiness. The baggage was loaded on board. Still Dr Leone did not tell them what he had been doing, though they burned with curiosity. He was making small talk and looking around as if he expected to see someone there. And then, quite suddenly, Ned gave a shout.

'It's them! It's the Tedeschis and Claudio! They've got bags with them! They must be coming with us on the ship to London!'

'Of course they are coming on the ship. And so am I,' said Dr Leone, flourishing a small bag. 'But not to London, though perhaps that might come later.' He laughed at the looks on their faces. 'We will ask the master of your good ship to drop us in one of the Adriatic ports closest to Greece—and from there take other ships and other conveyances till we find ourselves in Alexandria. Yes, Alexandria!' He gave Ned a clap on the shoulder. 'It was *your* words that pierced the melancholy fog in my mind, dear boy! Your words, about flying! It reminded me of how Miracolo, the flying alchemist, came from Alexandria, and how I've always wanted to go there—and how it is a place of many different sorts of people, living side by side and mingling. So I rushed over to Jacob's house and finally persuaded the stubborn doctor that I found the climate of Venice really very uncongenial now and planned to move to Alexandria; that I not only wanted their company on my trip there, but that I proposed to buy a large house there, and would be honoured if he might set up his physician's practice alongside my alchemist's study, and that his daughter and Claudio might make a life there together too, unmolested by spite and jealousy. And that if one was a Jew and one was a Christian, well, that was a question for God and not man.' He looked over at the Tedeschis, fast approaching. 'And it's to his sister Rachel I owe the final persuasion; for she as much as told her brother that if he was going to break his heart over a city corrupt to the marrow, then she, for one, was not going to stand by and let it happen. "We will go with you, Dr Leone," she said; "but as to the other proposal, we will make up our own minds." What a spirit! Fine-looking woman, but a bit of a tartar!'

'And more than a match for you, my friend,' said Matthew Ashby, laughing.

'Do you think so? I intend to show her I am in fact her match in every way,' said Dr Leone calmly. 'And I won't take no for an answer either.'

'I'm sure you won't,' snorted Bess Quickly, 'but it's whether she'll take the question, Orlando Leone!'

'Oh, I always get my way,' said the alchemist with a big smile as he hurried forward to help the ladies with their bags.

Much later, Ned, Celia, Sarah, and Claudio stood at the railings of the deck as the ship glided through the smooth, darkening water. The others were below, chattering over the remains of their meal. The four young people had been talking animatedly too, but now they were quiet, Ned's arm around Celia, and Claudio's around Sarah. Below them, the teeming sea heaved and glittered darkly; to one side of the ship they could just about glimpse land, but it was fading fast from view. Ned felt his love's heart beating close to him, her warmth becoming his warmth, a moment of perfect harmony that went to the core of his being. He thought of all that had happened. And suddenly, words came whispering into his head. *What profit love, that cannot show his face?*

Words that he knew for certain, without a doubt, were the beginning of something wonderful. A long poem—no, a play, telling a story stronger and stranger, more piteous and more beautiful too, than anything he had ever written before. A tragedy: a story of a great and passionate love, a love that survived death, that went through the very gates of hell . . . Not his story and Celia's, nor even Claudio and Sarah's, though there would be elements that stemmed from both of those, but the story of two young lovers called Edmund and Beatrice, who loved each other in Venice, long ago. It would be a story worth writing. It would be a memorial to those lost lovers, a beautiful story to make crowds weep. . . .

'What's the matter, Ned?' said Celia.

'Nothing,' he said, smiling at her. 'Nothing at all.'

'You were talking to yourself.'

'Was I, my love?' he answered teasingly.

'You were. I suppose you were thinking of something you wanted to write. A play?'

'Yes.'

'Aren't you going to tell me?'

He looked sideways at her. 'I thought you didn't like plays.'

'I've changed my mind about quite a few things,' said Celia serenely, strands of her hair blowing across her face. 'So maybe I can change my mind about that too. In fact, I might even go to the Globe with you next time you go.'

He laughed, and cuddled her closer, and told her what he was thinking. He even whispered to her the first four lines that had come fully formed to his head. She listened, her head on one side; then she said, 'I like it. It's real, Ned. It's like real life. Not like what . . . what you used to write.' A pause, then she went on, 'I think it will be a good play. I know what you should call it too. *The Lovers of Venice*.'

'Yes,' he said. 'Yes, Celia. I rather think you're right.' And in his mind rose an image of the stage at the Globe, and crowds cheering and weeping over *The Lovers of Venice*. And himself in the audience, with his family from London, and his friends from Venice, and especially Celia beside him, his muse, his lover, his dearest, sweetest friend. He could hear the crowds now and the music playing as the actors took their places on the stage. He could see the setting of the beautiful, golden, treacherous city; the gondolas plying, the masked throngs, the dark secrets behind the bright façade. And he murmured:

Now listen well, for here thou will be told
Of darkness, danger, and of lovers bold,
Of poison plots, of vengeance, and of love supreme,
In fairest Venice, where we set our scene.

Afterword

As you might already have realized, *The Madman of Venice* is inspired by two of Shakespeare's 'Italian' plays: *The Merchant of Venice,* of course, but also *Romeo and Juliet*. The first play, which was the first of Shakespeare's plays I ever encountered, and which struck me deeply, is also one of his most controversial. It is a dark story of revenge, full of ambiguous characters, especially the Jewish moneylender, Shylock, who's eaten away by hatred of the unjust Christians who persecute his people, but who is himself not a very nice sort of person at all.

Yet Shakespeare gives him one of his most famous speeches ever, a real cry from the heart:

> *'I am a Jew. Hath not a Jew eyes? Hath not a Jew hands, organs, dimensions, senses, affections, passions? Fed with the same food, hurt with the same weapons, subject to the same diseases, healed by the same means, warmed and cooled by the same winter and summer as a Christian is? If you prick us, do we not bleed? If you tickle us, do we not laugh? If you poison us, do we not die? And if you wrong us, shall we not revenge?'*
>
> (*The Merchant of Venice,* act 3, scene 1)

In the time when my book is set, the Jews of Venice held a special position in the city. They were better off than in most other places in Europe, because they were protected by law from outright persecution and violence. But they paid a pretty heavy price for that protection. They were forced to live on the island called the Ghetto. They had to wear special clothes that would mark them out as Jews. They could leave the Ghetto during the day but not at night—unless they were doctors—and they had to pay the wages of the Venetian guards who patrolled the Ghetto's borders at night. As well, they could only practise certain trades, including medicine, moneylending, and dealing in cloth, and they weren't allowed to own land. Of course, marriages between Jews and Christians were strictly forbidden unless the Jewish party converted, and even then they were regarded with great suspicion. And yet, despite all these difficult constraints, a rich and vital culture built up in the Venetian Ghetto, and even today you can see traces of that culture there.

I was also greatly inspired in my writing of this book by a visit I made to Venice in 2003. I fell in love at once with the beauty, strangeness, and unique atmosphere of this amazing city, floating serenely on its stone raft in the lagoon. And I was fascinated by its rich, deep, and disturbing history, with its sinister and enchanting aspects.

Incidentally, Emilia Lanier, who sends Ned and his friends off on their mission, was a real person. Her musician father, Baptista Bassano, came over to England from Venice with his equally musical brothers at the express invitation of King Henry VIII. Her mother, Margaret, was English and came from London, and she married Alfonso Lanier, another court musician. There is some evidence that the Bassanos may have been converted Jews, but no one's quite sure.

Like her father and husband, Emilia Lanier was an excellent musician, and played for Queen Elizabeth I. Highly intelligent, she was also a published poet, some of whose work still survives. She was a great beauty and very ambitious and was, for a while, the mistress of the Lord Chamberlain, Henry Carey, Lord Hunsdon. She is thought to have known Shakespeare, and it's possible he got some of his information about Italy from her, especially about Venice and the Veneto region, which includes Verona, where *Romeo and Juliet* and *The Two Gentlemen of Verona* are set. In fact, some people have even suggested that she was Shakespeare's lover at one stage and might have been the model for the mysterious 'Dark Lady' of Shakespeare's sonnets.

Sophie Masson was born in Jakarta, Indonesia, to French parents. The author of twenty-eight novels for adults, teenagers, and children, she is the winner of the Australian Aurealis Award for Best Children's Novel. She lives in New South Wales, Australia.